DAMAGE LIMITATION

by
N.M. YOUNG

ISBN 978-1-7384389-0-7

Cover design & typesetting by Raspberry Creative Type

Disclaimer:

This book is a product of the author's vivid imagination. Any resemblance to actual persons or cretins, living or dead, or to any actual events, is purely coincidental. To anyone who can see themselves in any of the more unsavoury characters, the author hopes that you might take time to reflect on your behaviour and become a better person. To anyone who is living with domestic abuse in any of its abhorrent forms, the author wishes you strength and fortitude for your journey. There is always hope.

1.

As DC Lucy Russell groggily opened her eyes, she could hear birds chirping over a background of city noise. She heard sounds of moving traffic, engines idling, people chatting and distant shouts. It was bright but her skin was cold and covered in goose bumps. She felt disorientated and had a creeping feeling that something wasn't right. She became aware that she was lying down, her back against a cold, solid surface and that she was fully clothed. Her right hand felt damp and gritty, the air was tainted with stale cigarette smoke. Eyes open and struggling to focus she became aware of sharp, urgent words in her ear and realised she wasn't in her bed, but sprawled on a city pavement. She turned her head to the side and saw a small group of taxi drivers across the road, their mouths open. Their attention was on her, a young woman lying flat on her back in the street outside a city bar. One of the men took a couple of steps towards her before being dissuaded by a well-meaning hand tugging his shirt sleeve, urging him to stay where he was and not to get involved.

A tall, agitated man stood over her. The watching taxi drivers correctly assumed this was the woman's boyfriend and this was a domestic situation. They had no appetite to get involved now. Too messy.

A police description of Detective Sergeant Danny Rae would have been: Male; white; forty three years old; five feet, ten inches tall; medium build; short, dirty-blonde hair, greying and thinning; grey-blue eyes; clean-shaven; sharp facial features. At this moment Danny's face was red and his scalp shiny with a slick of sweat. His features were pinched and angry-looking. His mouth a thin-lipped line, eyes blazing with fury.

'Get up now,' he hissed, bending so that his mouth was closer to her ear.

Lucy felt shocked with the sudden realisation that she was not waking up from a restful sleep but from a punch which had knocked her off her feet. She was twelve years younger than Danny and stood four inches shorter than him. Her small frame had been felled easily, especially by such an unexpected blow – a punch to the mouth. Her body had thumped down heavily on the unforgiving paving slabs, knocking the wind out of her as she landed. The back of her head had connected painfully with the solid surface, mixing shiny hair with blood and the grime and cold of the ground. She could smell traffic fumes and the putrid contents of a nearby bin.

Her head began to pound, the small cut at the bony part of her skull throbbing in protest. Panic and desperation took hold as she found herself unable to rise from the ground. She registered a stinging, sharp pain at the top left of her mouth. Probing the inside of her top lip gently with her tongue she found a cavity in the flesh, which corresponded to her canine tooth. She tasted the tang of blood in her mouth.

Rolling onto her side, Lucy sucked a mouthful of air as pain ran down the length of her right leg. Her right hip smarted, bringing tears to her eyes.

Feeling as if she had been run over, but knowing it wasn't true, her brain pieced together what had happened in the last few minutes. Lucy recalled that she and Danny had been at an afterwork gathering for a colleague who was leaving their division.

Lucy had carefully selected casual attire, mindful of Danny's jealous nature. She had worn a pair of relaxed-fit, dark-blue jeans paired with a loose-fitting, plain white t-shirt, and a pair of suede ankle boots; comfortable, stylish and suitable to run in should the need arise.

After what felt like several minutes, but was only seconds, Lucy's body complied enough to struggle into a sitting position. She gently felt the lump which was forming at the back of her head, her fingers came away bloodied. Danny was walking away but came back to stand over her again, fists clenching at his side. She wanted to ask him why he had done it, but there was no time for that now. Damage limitation kicked in instinctively. They had to get away from the area as quickly as possible, before anyone called for the police.

2.

Back at her office desk, face heavy with concealer and foundation, Lucy kept her head down. When asked about the swelling and bruising on her face, she hated having to tell a lie. Eyes downcast, she mumbled about a fault with the rowing machine at her gym. Roddy, the office clown, had sensed weakness and, probing for more detail, he made a big deal about how she should sue the gym.

Hiding behind a curtain of hair, Lucy handed out folders for Operation Flame to the assembled detectives, ready for the morning briefing. She was the Surveillance Operational Commander for the long-running drugs investigation centred in Aberdeen on an organised crime group headed by a ruthless father and son. Each file contained a synopsis of the operation, full nominal details, with photographs of the subject and all associates, along with intelligence on businesses, addresses and phone numbers.

They didn't have long to wait until Inchy barged into the office, the muster room door banging shut as he backheeled it with some force. The detective inspector clearly meant business this morning, not even taking time to remove his well-worn, tan leather jacket – his signature look. His opinions were as out of date as his fashion sense. He was not a popular man but he was still the boss and he liked to ensure they all remembered it. 'Inchy' had been named after a tiny cartoon detective character; his full nickname was Inch High DI.

What their DI lacked in height he more than made up for in formidable temper. Nobody liked to get on his wrong side. He spoke quickly, his sentences littered with swearing. A thick Highland accent became more pronounced as he became more infuriated, obliging his team to concentrate on his small, rapidly moving mouth under its thick moustache, in order to decipher the diatribe.

The squad were a select group of highly skilled detective officers from all over Scotland. On paper they were the best that each of the eight regions had to offer. Places were limited and sought after. There was plenty of banter among the team, especially after triumphs and defeats. It was usually harmless; well-intentioned and well-received. The jobs were difficult, often placing them in danger. It was a highly competitive environment full of big characters with bigger egos.

The team's administrative assistant, Caroline, was a long-serving civilian member of staff, nearing retirement. She had been in the role long enough to see dozens of detectives pass through. She was fond of saying that they all brought her joy – some when they walked into her office and some when they left. Caroline was a kind soul, soft-spoken and unassuming, but she had her wits about her and missed nothing. When Lucy had walked past her office that morning, Caroline had warned her that Inchy was in a foul mood.

Caroline had noticed her face but didn't allow her gaze to linger on the bruises. This small act of kindness made Lucy's eyes sting and she fought to remain composed. A kind word would have been the tipping point and started waterworks, which they both knew would do no good in that office.

At the briefing Inchy chewed a fingernail as he read a message on his mobile. 'Right, there's been a murder,' he said without even a flicker of irony. Pausing, he turned to Lucy and added, 'You need to come with me. We're going to Aberdeen to speak to the SIO. Operation Flame is on the back burner just now.' Getting up, he went to the door, still reading the message.

'Boss, what are we doing today then?' asked Roddy.

Still lost in his own thoughts and irritated by the sound of Roddy's voice, Inchy rounded on him, eyes blazing. 'Pick another one! Any job! Just get out,' he said, with his hand on the muster room door.

Lucy found Inchy sitting behind his desk, phone clamped between his ear and his shoulder, deep in conversation. He mimed opening a book and pointed at the door. When Lucy failed to guess the mime, he sighed, hurriedly scratched notes in a daybook and finished the call.

'Bring through the master file for Flame,' he told her. Looking up from his book, his eyes fell on the bruising to her face.

'What happened to you?'

Lucy blushed a deep red, formulating words for the gym-accident lie.

'Never mind. I don't have time for that,' he said.

For once Lucy was grateful for his lack of patience.

With the folder in front of him, Inchy leafed to the Associate section of Operation Flame, stopping at the entry for Lee Aitchison, son of their operational subject, Ralph Aitchison. He explained that a murder investigation was under way in Aberdeen after a male with an extensive criminal history, known mostly for drug-dealing, had been found dead in his home. Lucy asked if it had been confirmed as murder, prompting a curt reply, 'Well, there was a big kitchen knife sticking out his chest and his door had been booted in. So even the Aberdeen CID have worked that much out.'

She watched his face pinch as he explained that Lee Aitchison was suspected to be responsible. He told her that they would drive to Aberdeen and meet with the murder SIO, to see if there was anything they could add and find out what this meant in relation to Operation Flame.

'It's still hush, hush,' he told her.

Well used to the 'need-to-know' basis of information, Lucy only enquired who the SIO was.

'It's your dad. DCI Ian Russell. I considered taking someone else from your team, but since you're the ops commander for the drugs job, you're the one who knows it inside out.'

Lucy never shirked extra work or responsibility, regularly taking on the role of Ops Comm, enjoying the bonus of being able to pick her own team.

Lucy and Inchy walked into DCI Russell's office. 'Hello,' she said, in a general greeting to those gathered, giving a small smile and nod of acknowledgement to her father. Murder-team detectives filled them in on the circumstances, finishing with the description given to them of a male seen fleeing from the crime scene. The witness, one of the deceased's neighbours, had described a lingering smell of strong aftershave. They had managed to note part of a registration number and the colour, make and model of a car in which it was assumed that the killer had sped away in.

On the drive back to their own offices, Lucy and the DI discussed the likelihood of Lee Aitchison being the murderer. It seemed out of place for him to go hands-on. The victim had been stabbed multiple times – overkill. Why would Lee Aitchison deal with anyone so far down the food chain? His family business included drugs, but at a much higher level; larger-scale distribution, not just a few hundred pounds worth. If it was a debt, why hadn't Lee just used enforcers?

'They don't have enough to get him over the line yet and they know they'll only get one crack at him,' Inchy said. 'We're not ready to show our cards yet on Operation Flame, so they'll hold off for now while they do the groundwork CCTV trawls, ANPR and door-knocking, but we don't have long.'

'I get it,' Lucy said. 'They want to use us and our surveillance logs to link him with the getaway car and they're hoping we might gather evidence of conduct after the crime.'

'Yep, in a nutshell,' he agreed.

They would have probably been asked to assist in the murder case without the drugs link being there, Lucy supposed, remembering another case where the team had followed a murder suspect back to the shallow grave he had dug.

Lucy checked her watch, picked up her work phone and started to muster the troops for a briefing. Next, she picked up her own mobile and sent a text to Danny: *Job on. Sorry I'll be late home XX.*

Her screen blinked, then the reply came through: *Not again. I'm working with an old friend I'll just stay at his tonight.* After a short delay it was followed by a separate *XX.*

Danny had been working more nights lately. There was no time to dwell on her home situation, as Inchy brought the car to a clumsy halt and they went inside the squad's office.

As Lucy's team assembled, a low chatter started as they clucked like hens and fired questions at her. When Roddy found out who the SIO was, he started to chuckle and asked Lucy if there had been enough seats at the Aberdeen briefing, or had she had to sit on her dad's knee? She let the laughter die down and restored order to give the briefing, reminding everyone to cancel any plans for the next few days – they were in it for the long haul.

Inchy did not do well under pressure, but it did make him quiet, which was no bad thing. He didn't deploy with them, but they needed a supervisor on the ground for this one. Chewing at his nail, he spat a piece out on the grubby office carpet.

'Lucy, you'll be Ops Comm with DS Summers.'

Lucy was pleased she'd be working with Detective Sergeant Chris Summers. He was a tall, gangly football-mad gentleman. Well-liked and respected by the team, he was good at plugging the supervisory gaps left by Inchy. He also happily took his turn working on foot with surveillance teams or being cramped in the back of their anonymous van when needed.

Lucy called the team's analyst to help with the latest dump of data for Lee Aitchison. A load of telephone numbers, associated calls, messages and code words all waited to be sifted and might give them some clue as to Lee's current whereabouts, by identifying which address or with whom he might be lying low. Lucy unlocked her desk drawer, releasing a waft of overripe fruit as she pulled it open. Tossing a brown banana, the remains of a long-forgotten lunch, into the bin next to her desk, she lifted a pile of A4 pads and computer printouts ready to share with the analyst and logged on to her computer.

3.

The businesses and homes of associates already linked to Operation Flame had all been covertly checked for Lee Aitchison with negative result.

As expected, Lee had gone to ground. There was no sign of life at his home address but that was not unusual. He seldom spent time alone, preferring instead to hang about wherever he could find company – with lieutenants and underlings on the drug-dealing payroll or anyone at Ralph Aitchison's gentlemen's club. Lee frequently turned up at his father's club towards closing time ready for some alcohol and a few lines. He would sniff out a private party or slip away with one of the dancers eager for his attention.

Lucy was back at the squad's office, liaising with the data analyst when her mobile rang. DS Chris Summers' name flashed on the screen – an update from the field.

'It might be a nobody, but we've got a new player here,' he told her. 'I'm sending you the image.'

A ping came from her desk computer as the grainy image arrived. The photograph had been taken from a distance. Blurred, it didn't show much detail, but she could see a tall, muscular, heavily built male, probably in his early thirties. He had ducked into the club well before opening hours, with a mobile phone clamped to his ear.

'Yes, he's new and he doesn't look like a dancer.' Lucy sucked air through her teeth. She and Chris discussed whether to follow the male, hoping to identify him. With any luck he might even lead them to Lee.

'Okay, let's go with him,' she agreed, terminating the call.

Lucy sighed, turning back to the pile of telephone records. She had been checking to see whether any of the numbers they had for Lee Aitchison had been active near the East-End murder scene in Aberdeen at the right time. She now started afresh, trying to find a number they could link to the new face.

Later that day the team gathered to run through the day's logs and shared information. As they debriefed, DS Chris Summers passed round images of the unidentified male. Lucy took her turn, sifting through the printed image sheets, stopping at one, holding it closer to inspect the clearest photograph. The navy-blue Hugo Boss jeans and black Stone Island jacket he wore suggested he came from further up the drug-dealing staff list. These were part of an unofficial uniform providing distinction from the Adidas-clad small fry and their customers. Any criminal worth their salt could spot a plain-clothes police officer a mile away – North Face and Superdry were their current brands of choice; they might as well wear a police uniform. Thanks to the surveillance job, Lucy's own wardrobe had become as bland as her social life. It was easier to blend in, not to stick out, with no obvious labels, bright colours or patterns.

Still studying the image, Lucy listened to Chris as he described the events which had led to their unidentified male being lost from sight in heavy traffic and not seen again that day. The car he had been driving was a black Audi A4, one they had not seen on the plot previously. It had the look of a 'pool car' about it, an unremarkable motor which would be passed round and used by the gang. All the driver had to do was keep it in a straight line, stick more or less to the speed limits and they would be pretty much invisible to the police. Common looking, legitimate enough and apparently legal, it would pass a basic roadside check if they were stopped by the police.

'Chris,' she said suddenly, still peering at the image in her hand, 'I know who this is.'

Lucy regarded the face of her primary-school classmate Robbie Gillies. She recalled the last conversation she had had with her mother who enthused about Robbie having 'landed on his feet' with a highly paid job somewhere in the offshore industry. Robbie's mother had bragged about him choosing expensive wallpaper, having a new luxury flat in the city centre decorated to his taste. It seemed that his sudden change of fortune and wealth was not from a job offshore after all, but from being involved in some part of the Aitchison drug racket. She didn't know how he had made the jump from small-town jobbing labourer and apple of his mother's eye to hanging with that crowd, but perhaps a chance meet at his gym and plenty of cash being thrown about had been enough. She was surprised – he genuinely did not seem to be the career-criminal type.

Lucy declared her involvement. Even though they had only seen each other in passing as adults, he would easily recognise her on the street and already knew she was a police officer – enough to spook him if she was seen. Lucy would have to be kept out of his sight, probably doing more back-office roles on the phones or in an airless surveillance van.

'We can pick him up from his mum's house,' Lucy told them. 'I believe he has a flat somewhere in the city, apparently it's being redecorated.'

Agreeing a plan for the next day, Lucy volunteered to

take the van. 'I'll easily be able to spot Robbie whenever he appears.'

At the end of her shift, Lucy yawned and stretched in the chair. Switching off the computer, she adhered to a strict 'clear-desk' policy and locked away all paperwork before heading home to her empty flat.

Lucy's stomach rumbled on the drive home, reminding her that she had missed lunch. Checking the time, she decided to pick up a takeaway and worked out that she wouldn't have enough time for the bath she wanted. She would make do with a quick shower then get off to bed and back into the office as early as possible the next morning so they could be ready for the target before he started his day. She was back on the hamster wheel of work, sleep, work. No wonder she had no time to meet up with friends or have hobbies – she couldn't even keep up with her dentist. She had called to cancel another dental appointment earlier in the week while on a train, following a drugs courier.

Lucy's phone vibrated in her pocket with a series of text-message alerts as she drove. Several more arrived before she parked in the space allocated to her flat. Still sitting in the driver's seat, she scrolled through them. Her friend and former colleague Detective Sergeant Fiona Cunningham had sent a series of messages in a one-sided conversation, wondering if she would like to join her on a short break to Rome. There were details of flights, accommodation and some random Italian words. Nothing from Danny, but he would probably still be working, she thought, as she dashed off a message let him know that she was back at home for the night and free to take a call from him if he could manage. Walking in to the cool, dark flat she smelled fading lilies from the lounge as she juggled keys and a plastic bag of Chinese food, taking her personal and work phones off silent mode to ensure she didn't miss a call from Danny, or an urgent update about the operation. Opening a carton of cooling chow mein, Lucy fished out the complimentary disposable fork. Not bothering with a plate, she stirred and poked at the mass.

Swallowing a mouthful of noodles, Lucy lifted her ringing work mobile, seeing that the caller ID was Chris Summers. Alert again, she answered it, half-expecting to be called back into the office. There was no update on Lee Aitchison's whereabouts but the background checks on Robbie Gillies were in. They now had two mobile numbers tied to him and both were active.

Lucy chased congealing noodles about the takeaway container with the bendy plastic fork as they discussed the murder investigation. There was no new intelligence, but Forensics were still working on the locus with plenty still to do. Motive for the killing was not yet known. With the mobile phone jammed between her shoulder and ear, Lucy awkwardly binned the takeaway container and began opening kitchen-cabinet doors. Neither she nor Danny had done any shopping lately. There wasn't even milk in the fridge.

Lucy sat back down at the small kitchen table with a cup of instant black coffee and a box of French Fancies, the sweet cakes more appealing than the cold takeaway. She and Chris debated what the motive could be for Lee Aitchison to commit murder. The deceased had definite drugs connections to Operation Flame and had been a small-scale dealer, selling enough heroin to fund his own increasing habit. He had shifted a few bags to his own circle of friends and their friends but had been at the bottom of the Adidas league. They still couldn't work out why the strictly designer-clad Lee would put his hands on the victim when he had plenty of foot soldiers to do his dirty work.

Why had he been alone on the visit when it was always risky making a house call? Weapons would be kept out of sight, but close at hand, easily recovered if the occupant felt threatened, aggrieved or was just high. There were a few regular visitors to the locus, but no drugs were stashed there; deals were done on the street around the corner. There was no way the victim could have run up the kind of debt that would bring an Aitchison to his home. He was the desperate kind of addict; one of those who was the reason health centres had to fix bottles of hand sanitiser to their walls. He would have taken anything to knock the edge off the desperate cravings when they came. Absent-mindedly, Lucy put another French Fancy in her mouth, washing it down with too-hot coffee. No wonder the SIO hadn't written off the murder as a drugs debt. It didn't fit the profile, Chris and Lucy agreed, as they ended the call.

Lucy got up, yawning and went to the front door to retrieve the mail she'd stepped over on her way in. A few bits of junk mail, a flyer for a new pizza place and a plain envelope with what felt like a bank card inside. It was addressed to Danny. She binned everything apart from the envelope containing the card, which she propped up on the table. Its arrival would save Lucy the hassle of having to lend him hers and the constant need to carry cash. They had set up a joint bank account when they had agreed the flat lease, and £55,000 – Lucy's savings – had been deposited to open the account. They had intended to set up a savings account, but hadn't made time to do something so mundane, preferring to spend their limited time off together, having fun. Only Lucy's wages were currently paid into their joint account, until Danny's legal separation or divorce was settled. He had told her that he wanted to do the right thing by his family, to keep paying into his estranged wife's account so that she and the children could remain in their home until it was sold. Lucy had agreed that some continuity for Susan and the children was a small price to pay. They could live on her wages and savings in the meantime but Danny was proving to be expensive to keep.

Lucy messaged Danny, letting him know his bank card had arrived and that she was going to bed for an early start. Looking at the clock she reckoned she would manage a solid five hours' sleep before she had to get up and do it all again.

4.

The team was still trying to locate murder suspect, Lee Aitchison, who was proving hard to find. Covert human intelligence sources had been primed; secrets were hard to keep in the drugs world. Somebody would eventually be desperate enough to give up the information they needed, 'grassing' for a small fee to buy their next fix.

It turned out that Robbie Gillies's role was that of an enforcer. He had muscle and a menacing look, which the Aitchison empire had recognised as useful to control loose lips and drug debts. Robbie now had more money than he knew what to do with. He was sensible enough not to go blowing it all in one place or in one showroom. No point having his mother, or the police ask questions he didn't want to answer. Gambling and visiting the lap-dancing bar owned by Ralph Aitchison were his regular pastimes. Even with a hefty discount he still put away hundreds each night on overpriced, under-chilled drinks and the dancers. Lee Aitchison had demonstrated how to flaunt wealth and use swagger to impress the ladies. Robbie had soon developed his own confidence, getting a taste for the performers. He enjoyed the ego boost of them flirting with him. At first, he had been flattered by all the attention from the skinny girls but then he had seen them take a line or two of cocaine between their routines before turning the same gaze to the next punter, hungry for money, not time.

Ralph and Lee Aitchison liked having Robbie hang around the bar when he was not needed elsewhere. It kept the punters in line when they saw him chat to the bouncers, dwarfing them in the dimly lit doorframe as he flexed and cracked his knuckles. It also saved having to send messages and make calls, which they were acutely aware could be intercepted by the permanently circling police – not all of them could be paid to look the other way. Ralph Aitchison regularly complained that it was not like the days of old, when a couple of the big police bosses had been regulars and a few snapshots of their drunken antics inside private dance booths had been enough to keep them bent.

Ralph Aitchison sat hunched at his desk, number crunching while a cleaner noisily emptied the wastebin next to him. His lips thinned over gritted teeth as the lead tip of his mechanical pencil snapped and pinged onto the floor. He placed the pencil on his desk with too much care. He rested his elbows on the desk, fists balled at his mouth and he bit the knuckle of his right hand. Closing his eyes tightly he reminded himself that he was no longer locked up in a prison cell. Loud noises took him back there, set his teeth on edge and made his heart hammer. Now the cleaner sprayed furniture polish and the smell caught the back of his throat. He rubbed his temples, got up, grabbed his jacket and made for the door. Lee met him in the narrow corridor, the bulk of him blocking his path. Ralph stared at him, 'Get out the way.'

Lee smirked, standing his ground, looking his father up and down. Ralph took a determined step forward. Lee watched him, arms straight at his side, tense. After an awkward second, Lee lifted his right arm, causing Ralph to flinch involuntarily and his cheeks to colour.

'Alright, old man.' Lee spoke, patting him on the shoulder and moving aside, grinning now.

Ralph looked back towards the office, pressing his fist into his thigh, at least they were alone. He straightened and looked Lee in the eye, pulling himself to his full height which despite subtly elevated shoes was still a couple of inches shorter than his son. He walked past, stumbling slightly and swearing at the carpet.

Lee had enjoyed being top dog, running the business in Ralph's absence. He cut an imposing figure: built up on steroids to fill his tight shirts and trousers, he thought himself well above the saps who consumed the heroin and cocaine they sold. Sure, he would have a few lines himself, but he wouldn't touch the smack, and that, for him, was the definitive line between him and the rest. He smiled slyly, if Ralph was sent down again it might be better if he didn't get out.

Lucy hugged DS Fiona Cunningham as she walked into the muster room.

'Long time no see,' she told her old friend.

'So, are you coming to Rome?' Fiona asked as she shrugged off her jacket, digging in a well-worn satchel for her laptop and daybook.

'Probably not, I've got too much on just now,' Lucy replied.

DS Chris Summers joined them and they briefed Fiona on the enquiry as she clicked on the laptop and questioned them in finer detail. Fiona and Lucy had already worked together on Operation Flame, making inroads with some of the sex workers in Aberdeen. Like drug-users, dealers and the police, they had their own hierarchy and street workers were at the bottom. Sometimes these workers, mostly women, had a handler or pimp who syphoned off their earnings. Often it was their significant other – husband, boyfriend, or whatever. Most were independent or self-employed, with their own patch, usually near the harbour, where they waited to be collected by passing cars.

Then there were the dancers. Public-facing, they worked in bars like those belonging to the Aitchisons. They were paid an attractive wage even after the club took deductions to pay for overheads and security, feeling safer at work with the no-touching rule enthusiastically enforced by bored bouncers and doormen.

Escorts were the next level. A few started in clubs before being offered more money to work fewer shifts at private parties or orgies in an apartment or house rented by the Aitchisons or their peers. The venues changed swiftly before snobby neighbours became fed up with the flow of taxis and visitors and alerted the authorities.

Chris slapped his palms on his thighs. 'Right then, I'll see if your car has arrived.'

Lucy and Fiona followed Chris out the office, collecting keys for a Renault Clio hire car. They were going to visit one of Fiona's sources, a street girl, and they didn't want to risk her safety by using Fiona's unmarked CID car with its easily recognisable double ariel and sequential numberplate. By treading lightly, they gained trust and could help each other. These women were the eyes and ears of the city, underrated and underestimated by their clients and their partners.

Fiona made a couple of calls, arranging to meet 'Destiny' on her patch. Checking her watch, she told Lucy they had half an hour to kill. Lucy agreed to drive Fiona to the back door of Marks and Spencer's and waited patiently, checking her phone while Fiona grabbed a bag of groceries. Danny had left a voicemail letting her know that he had picked up his bank card and was on his way to take his children out for dinner. She could hear their excited chatter in the background. Smiling, she ended the call and Fiona climbed in the car.

When they turned onto the appointed street at the appointed time to meet Destiny it was empty. Rolling her eyes, Fiona told Lucy to keep driving and park at the nearby leisure centre.

'We'll give it twenty minutes and try again. These lassies work even more unpredictable hours than us,' she said, leaning into the rear footwell to grab a packet of sandwiches from a carrier bag. Twenty minutes later, Destiny was in the expected place. She climbed hurriedly into the back seat as soon as they stopped.

'Move it,' she said, sliding down in the seat, filling the car with the scent of cheap, liberally applied perfume.

They found a safe place to park away from prying eyes. 'M&S,' Destiny said, using what she thought was a good impression of the television advert voiceover as she rooted through the contents of the carrier bag. 'Nice.'

'Get off,' Fiona told her, reaching over to flap the bag closed.

As the chat moved on to business, Destiny moaned that she wouldn't be able to retire on the pittance she was paid as a police informant. Eyeing a row of bitten down nails, she told them the only reason she was cooperating was that Fiona had been dependable so far and that she wanted the scumbag who'd hurt her friend to pay for what he'd done.

Lucy and Fiona listened as Destiny told them about her friend, one of Ralph Aitchison's lap dancers, who had been suspected of skimming earnings from them. She described how her friend had been offered a lift home at the end of her shift by Lee Aitchison and another bloke called Roddy, or Robbie. Instead of taking her home they had driven her miles out of town to an old holiday park. Panicking, she had pleaded with them to let her go, but they'd dragged her into an abandoned caravan and tied her up. Lee had been high, shouting and spitting in her face about *his* money. The other guy had tried to stop it but there had been no calming Lee down. Destiny shivered despite the warmth of the car, telling them how Lee had made the other man burn the soles of her friend's feet with a blowtorch. Bile rose in Lucy's throat. She had absolutely no doubt that Destiny was speaking truthfully. In the end Lee and the other male, who from the description, was likely to be Robbie Gillies, had untied the woman, thrown her mobile phone at her, and left her in the caravan, in agony but alive. They had made sure she couldn't earn any money for long enough to teach her a lesson and knew word would spread among the rest of the dancers, keeping them all in line.

As Lucy drove Destiny back to her post, she regarded her in the rear-view mirror. Skinny, with long dirty-blonde hair scraped back into a ponytail, greasy tendrils framing her elfin face, she had dark circles under her eyes, visible under thick, poorly matched foundation. She had skin so pale it was almost transparent. Lucy asked Destiny when she last had a meal, she let out a bitter chuckle, showing stumps of blackened teeth, saying that eating 'wasn't her thing'. Dropping her off a couple of streets away, Lucy fished in the carrier bag behind her, then handed Destiny some sandwiches, a packet of chocolate biscuits and an energy drink.

'Hey!' said Fiona, in half-hearted protest.

'Thanks,' Destiny said as she climbed out. Turning to Fiona, she jabbed a thumb towards Lucy, 'You could learn some manners from that one.' Then shaking her head, she muttered, 'I wouldn't have your job for all the money in the world,' before closing the door and disappearing.

Lucy pulled away, telling Fiona, 'We need to get our hands on Robbie. I reckon he'll be the weak link.'

5.

Robbie Gillies pondered his current situation. In the films and television programmes he'd seen, police interview rooms had fancy mirrors with a couple of grim-faced detectives watching from behind the reflection. Robbie sat on a lopsided chair, foam stuffing spilling from the wipe-clean, shiny seat pad, in a room which was smaller than a cell. The walls needed a fresh coat of paint. He wondered if they had once been white but had been stained by years of cigarette smoking. Not so much magnolia-coloured walls, more like 'fag-nolia' he thought humourlessly. There were no smoking signs on the walls and on the back of the door, but he guessed they were just for show since he could smell remnants of cigarette smoke hanging in the airless room. He was a non-smoker but preferred the smell of cigarettes to the underlying aroma of cheesy feet and aftershave, which made him want to gag. Glancing down at his own stocking feet, Robbie flexed his toes, missing the shoes which had been taken from him by the custody officer when he was booked in. He wondered how many unwashed socks had roamed the grubby, threadbare carpet before him.

Robbie had been left alone for a few minutes, giving him time to study the large recording device which sat dormant at the end of the table. Looking up he saw a

CCTV camera in the corner of the ceiling and squirmed in his seat. He had run out of things to look at in the interview suite when he heard the clip-clop of approaching shoes. He sat up and watched the door expectantly.

Robbie looked anxiously into the faces of the two detectives in matching suits, who now sat across the table from him with competing aftershaves. The most overpowering scent came from the one sitting directly opposite him and coated the inside of his dry mouth.

Robbie had been a satisfyingly good burst for the detectives, when he had eventually rubbed his white knuckles over dry lips, and going against the 'no comment' telephone advice of his solicitor, admitted to driving without a licence. He knew that Ralph and Lee Aitchison would go spare, but figured he had no choice since he was going to be charged whether he coughed to it or not.

This had seemed to loosen his tongue. When they'd asked him about the assault on the dancer at the caravan, he'd allowed his conscience to win, telling them he deeply regretted his involvement and agreeing to be driven to the disused site, to point out the caravan they had used. He denied at first that Lee Aitchison had been there, worried that the solicitor, paid for by Ralph Aitchison, would report back to him and he would pay a fatal price for speaking up. When the detective had said he knew Robbie was lying and pointed out that they would find both their prints all over the caravan anyway, Robbie sat forward in the wonky chair, elbows on his shaking knees, and ran his hands through his hair.

He was in too deep with the Aitchison clan. His stomach churned with the realisation that he couldn't escape them. He'd heard all the stories from Lee about what a psychopath his uncle John was and how even his mother was frightened of her own brother. When he had met John, Robbie had the chilling feeling that he had met a monster and that the stories were more than just urban myth.

Robbie had concentrated on keeping on Ralph and Lee's good side. He should have disclosed his driving ban when he'd first started on the Aitchison payroll. He knew Ralph wouldn't like it, but the longer he worked for them, the more awkward it was to admit. His lack of driving licence had been the result of a drunken mistake one rainy night out in Edinburgh, when he couldn't find a taxi to get back to his digs. He'd managed to clip a parked car right outside St Leonard's police station. They hadn't even needed a police car; they had just walked him to the cells. Robbie hadn't felt the need to tell Ralph Aitchison, considering it trivial compared to what they did for a living. But Ralph knew better. He insisted that all his employees had licences, were insured and were always sober behind the wheel. On several occasions this had saved their cars from being seized when the police went through one of their irritating phases of disruption, frequently stopping them and checking them out.

Robbie worked more furiously at his hair as he realised how angry Ralph would be when he found out about his afternoon at the police station with the pair of matching CID officers. Robbie wasn't stupid. He knew the CID wouldn't be interested in his driving ban. He'd been stopped in the Audi by beat cops in their marked car, but as soon as he was booked into the custody suite they'd melted away and the bookend detectives had appeared, a sure sign they were after him for something more serious. Assault? Drugs? Racking his brain, he'd tried to pick out the worst of his crimes and prepare himself mentally for their line of questioning.

When they told him that he'd been under surveillance and mentioned the caravan, he had almost thrown up in their silly little metal dustbin at the side of the table. He had no poker face. The solicitor had insisted that he would be joining Robbie as soon as he could, despite his protestations that there really was no need. He had thought it strange how keen he was to visit him at the police station until he considered that he was just another one of Ralph's associates, making sure he knew what information the police had. Realising he wouldn't have long until his solicitor – or rather Ralph's solicitor arrived – he had given the bookends a little information, then asked to go back to his cell until their boss could speak to him. He wanted to save his skin. He didn't fancy his chances in any prison, not when Ralph was so well connected and so many inmates had nothing to lose. He was careful not to divulge too much to the bookends. Just enough to make it obvious that he really did have quality information, the kind to hopefully keep him out of jail. His palms were sweaty as he waited it out in the little cell with grubby walls, in no doubt that Ralph had connections in the force too. He needed to make sure he spoke to the right police officer if he was to try to get his life back.

Robbie had been charged with road traffic offences in the presence of his solicitor, and then to keep up appearances, had been asked if he knew anything about drug deals or assaults involving the Aitchisons. He had given 'no comment' replies to those questions in front of the solicitor, but his left eye had developed a twitch and he had almost burst into nervous laughter.

After what felt like an eternity to him, Robbie stood on the front steps of the police station gulping fresh air. He was as satisfied as he could be that the solicitor had no idea he had already betrayed the Aitchisons before his arrival but Robbie's hands shook as he stuffed court paperwork for driving offences into the pocket of his jacket.

He swallowed hard, switched his phone on and it immediately rang.

'Where the fuck are you?' Ralph Aitchison growled down the line.

6.

Lucy placed her fork on the elegant, gold-edged plate and studied Danny's eager face in soft candlelight. He had been trying hard over the last few days to make up for the time he had been working away from home. Long working hours and extra miles commuting back and forth to their flat left little time to socialise. She assumed that was the reason Danny had booked the overpriced Italian restaurant.

Lucy inhaled the rich cherry aroma of her red wine, her eyes already heavy with the effect of alcohol and the cosy atmosphere.

'Open that,' he pushed a plain white envelope over the crisp linen tablecloth towards her. He grinned.

'Tickets?' Lucy said, peering inside.

'We're going to Rome' he said simply and signalled to the waiter that he wanted another bottle of wine.

'But Fiona wants to go to Rome with me,' Lucy said gently, still smiling but eyeing Danny for any change in his demeanour. She was trying to forget it, but couldn't help being wary of him now after the sudden, explosive assault on her.

She had become accustomed to his impulsive, over-the-top gestures and gifts, but he understood that she'd hoped to take a trip away with her friend. She had intended to book it as soon as work quietened down enough to allow plans to be made, reasoning that she could pay for the trip with some of the overtime she was making on the current murder enquiry and drugs operation. She had learned to consider her words carefully when they talked, especially when he had been drinking, and was trying not to dwell on the fact that within a couple of months, Danny had steadily emptied their drinks cabinet. She hadn't bothered to restock any of it, preferring to keep alcohol out of their home.

When she had eventually made it home from work one night, he had startled her when she walked into the dark lounge. She had a habit of not bothering to switch on lights, navigating her home by memory. Her heart thumped and she balled a fist with her keys, when she saw a figure seated in a chair, glass in hand, blankly staring at her.

'Danny! You nearly gave me a heart attack,' she said, clicking on the lamp to reveal an empty bottle of brandy and the last of the expensive white wine she had been given as a birthday present and was saving for a special occasion. When he didn't speak, she asked him where his car was since she hadn't seen it in the car park. Danny just tapped the side of his nose, remaining silent and smirking. It had a most unnerving effect, especially when combined with his alcohol-soaked state.

'Got to keep you on your toes,' he said. Then added slyly, 'Just in case you had someone else round.'

'What?' she had never considered choosing someone else over him. They were in an exclusive, committed relationship and she wasn't remotely interested in anybody else. She had wanted to say that she hardly even saw her friends these days, but she didn't want to push him into the familiar stinging tirade about how she preferred to spend time with her friends rather than him, that she was bound to leave him, she was all he had left in the world and that he missed his children. In the end, he had got up, walked past her, a little unsteady on his feet and gone to bed, leaving her behind. She had dismissed the strange behaviour, putting it down to him being under pressure at work and stressed by his estranged wife having cancelled his weekend plans with the children, but it disturbed her.

These days, when sober, he was the same positive, happy person she had first fallen for, but when he took a drink, she had no way of telling whether he might morph into a sad, nasty drunk or the almost manic, impulsive version of himself who seemed to be sitting in front of her now.

Cautiously, Lucy suggested that perhaps they should not dip into their savings, deliberately not referring to the money as *hers*. The rented flat was supposed to be a short-term solution until Danny's house had been sold and they could join finances, purchasing somewhere together once they had found the ideal location. Danny went quiet and shovelled food bitterly into his mouth. Lucy instantly regretted saying anything. She felt guilty to have spoiled the moment, to have stolen his happiness. She felt her chest tighten. She didn't want anything more to drink, knowing instinctively that she needed to keep a clear head.

Lucy put a hand over her half-full wineglass, indicating to the waiter that she didn't want a top-up from the second bottle. With a weak smile, Lucy muttered her thanks, as she looked at two tickets for a flight to Rome. Danny was still quiet, shooing the waiter away impatiently and pouring wine to the top of his glass. A sour expression settled on his face, and Lucy fidgeted nervously in her seat. Unconsciously, she regarded the other diners, who appeared oblivious to them. They couldn't see what she did – the change of atmosphere and dark clouds gathering overhead.

Swallowing a lump in her throat and plastering on a fake smile, Lucy tried to lift the mood again. She accepted Danny's gift graciously, telling him how much she wanted to see the city, listing places they could visit. After a few minutes of one-sided enthusiasm, she was relieved to see Danny's shoulders drop. He sat back, looking at her, glass held midway to his mouth, then smiled. Lucy let out a breath of relief and the knot in her stomach untied. Why was she being so ungrateful when her partner had done such a lovely thing? He was only trying his best, arranging a holiday to a place he knew she wanted to visit. She reasoned that they would have plenty of time to top up their savings and he needed the break. Lucy tried hard to push aside her nagging doubts along with the plate of half-eaten food, thinking she just needed to go with the flow. Her appetite had disappeared and she glanced at her watch.

'Am I boring you?' he asked, a hard edge to his voice. She froze, not able to meet his eyes. Her muscles tightened again, she swallowed and her knee trembled under the table.

7.

Robbie Gillies' city-centre flat was a new build in a beautiful riverside location. The views from his lounge and master bedroom were to die for. He wasn't allowed to forget that it was a company benefit. He had frequent visitors from the drug-dealing side of the Aitchisons' business. He didn't know all of them and preferred to be kept in the dark, believing that ignorance was bliss. People he had never seen before arrived just after Ralph or Lee and were obviously known to them, invited round for secret meetings. When strangers arrived unexpectedly, Robbie asked a few 'security' questions then let them in.

He didn't like the late-night or middle-of-the-night visits from Lee Aitchison and his cronies. They made noise, brought drugs and girls round, using the place as their party pad. He had to pretend not to care when they were rowdy, drunk or high, spilling drinks and food all over the place, keeping him up when he just wanted to be left in peace to go to bed. Robbie had naively thought the place was his gift, rent-free in exchange for him being constantly on hand, even out of hours.

At first the visits had been sporadic, but they soon became so frequent that he felt as if he was running more of a club than Ralph was. He had no idea who would knock on his door next or when that would be, but he was always supposed to let them in and be a great host. There was an expectation that he should have ready supplies of beers and spirits and never mind that they outstayed their welcome, sometimes remaining overnight. The worst kind of visits were when Lee or Ralph Aitchison called round, agitated and short-tempered one minute, then all smiles and backslaps the next. Their unpredictable and violent natures made it impossible for him to relax when in their company. Often, they would ask Robbie for drinks and cigars, then look him up and down, making him feel awkward, until he realised he had been dismissed. Sometimes they asked him to fetch takeaway food, to get him out of the way for a while, but often he was just expected to clear out of his own home while they held meetings. It was exhausting.

The shine had soon worn off the luxury apartment for Robbie, who was not allowed to invite any of his old friends or his family round. He wouldn't have done anyway in case the lie about a well-paid job offshore was found out. He longed for the relative boredom of the modest bedroom at his mother's house and his old, simple life. By the time he had realised he was in the wrong line of business, he was in so deep with Ralph and Lee Aitchison that he couldn't see a way back.

At least the police had made an appointment to visit his flat, Robbie thought, as the detective walked past him, followed by someone who was introduced to him as a 'tech guy', but looked like a teenage gamer. Beads of sweat began to roll down Robbie's broad back.

'Please be quick,' Robbie said, as they wandered through the apartment, power tools in hand, closely examining ceilings, light fittings, wall sockets and ornaments, debating the best locations to hide their covert digital recording devices. Robbie paced back and forth at the lounge window, keeping an anxious lookout for any sign of the gang approaching his place. It was still early in the morning, which made visits unlikely since he doubted any of them would even be up yet, but he couldn't be entirely sure. Lee Aitchison was still hiding from the police, so surely if he was going to call round, he would pick the quietest time when nobody else was about. Robbie moved closer to the window, on high alert. Having the copper and the 'tech guy' in his flat gave him palpitations and he felt light-headed.

If Ralph or Lee Aitchison found out he was working for the other side he would have signed his own death warrant. But the desperate need to escape them was even greater than his fear and the police had assured him this was a sure-fire way to put them behind bars. He had been told that he would be protected, and his only reservation had been that he could never see or communicate with his mother again if push came to shove.

'Jesus!' the detective said to Robbie. 'I thought you said the place had just been decorated?' Turning slowly for the full effect, he took in the tan-coloured, chequered pattern of the carpet, matching wallpaper, curtains and bedlinen.

'If I was wearing a Burberry shirt in here, you'd never see me,' he said, shaking his head at the decor. 'I should be charging you with assault on my eyeballs.'

Robbie said nothing, picturing instead the torn posters of footballers, bands and gigs, which were still tacked to the bedroom wall at his mother's house.

A few minutes later his unwanted guests left, and Robbie ran around his flat like a demented cleaner, vacuuming and dusting to ensure that no telltale powdery trace of plaster or disturbed dust from their visit remained. He tried to ignore the bugs in his home, rubbing the back of his neck and thinking that he was a contestant in the grimmest reality show imaginable.

After a couple of days, just as he was beginning to forget his flat was wired straight to the police, he was forced to contact the detective again, pleading with him to fix whatever problem was causing his television to randomly change channel. As soon as the officers switched on the device at their end, his television went haywire. He had shrugged it off the first couple of times, blaming the dodgy Skybox he had bought from a chancer in the club. He had to swallow down panic when it happened again just as one of Lee's mates had called round to watch a fight on TV and empty his fridge of beers. Luckily, he had believed the dodgy box story, but Robbie reckoned he had lost about ten years of his life from the stress of it.

Lee Aitchison still had not resurfaced or been in touch with him. He'd heard rumours from nefarious visitors that he would be hiding out in Spain or somewhere in the North Sea aboard a trawler. Even Ralph didn't seem to know where his son was. Come to think of it, Robbie didn't think Ralph seemed to care very much about his son's absence.

8.

Lucy had felt guilty asking DS Chris Summers if she could take some time off for the trip to Rome. It was bad timing, right in the middle of the ongoing murder and drugs surveillance operations – especially when she was the operational commander. Chris had been great about it though, pointing out that things had slowed down and there were no current leads to locate Lee Aitchison. He would keep an eye on it until she got back. It was only a long weekend away and she had more than six weeks of annual leave waiting to be used. She hadn't taken time off for ages, always waiting for a quiet spell which never arrived. Danny had forced her hand by booking the tickets and hotel and she supposed that she should be thankful but was conflicted, wishing she could change the dates.

'Bring me back a stick of rock,' Chris said.

'I don't know if they sell it,' Lucy laughed.

'Bring me back some pasta then.'

As soon as they checked in their bags, Danny led the way to the airport bar. It wasn't even breakfast time yet and Lucy swallowed down yawns as he ordered a drink for each of them at the bar. It was a bit early for alcohol, she thought, but she didn't want to ruin the moment or bring down Danny's good mood by asking for an orange juice or coffee instead. The vodka was too sharp as she took a sip, watching a member of the bar staff walk up to their table with a wine cooler. Lucy opened her mouth, ready to tell them that it was a mistake, but Danny said, 'Put it there, mate', and she understood that he must have ordered it.

'Champagne to kick off a great holiday,' he enthused, pouring two glasses, handing the first to Lucy. Disguising a sigh of resignation with a weak smile, she clinked glasses, then checked her phone for messages. Nothing from Chris and nothing else that couldn't wait for a couple of days. Tucking it away, Lucy made a conscious effort to unclench her teeth and to make the most of the imposed break, forgetting about work for a few days.

As soon as they had found their seats on the aeroplane, Danny sat down heavily, next to the window. He was excited and happy in a childish way, and when he was like that, it was easy to be carried along on a wave of optimism, having fun together again. Before the plane had even begun to roll towards the runway, Lucy looked up from her magazine to see his head was already tilted back, his eyes were closed, mouth open and he was snoring quietly. She shook her head and carefully folded away his tray before settling back into her seat. Muscles relaxed as unconscious tension melted away. Her limbs felt pleasantly heavy as she took a deep breath in, sighed contentedly, and sank drowsily into the fug of a lack of sleep and plenitude of alcohol.

Lucy's eyes lazily followed the cabin crew as they ran through the preflight safety briefing, letting her mind run free. She wondered if she was able to properly relax because Danny was settled and content. She automatically put his needs before her own, trying to keep him on an even keel, but it was becoming more challenging to buoy him up. His dark moods were getting worse, she hoped they were caused by the stress he was under with his estranged wife and the pressures of work, but a small voice at the back of her head nagged that there would always be some difficulties in life, and there was no excuse for flying off the handle.

She regularly overheard tense telephone calls when Susan, his ex, complained that he needed to spend more time with their children, only to suddenly change her plans and spoil his chance to see them. Lucy tried her best to stay out of their disagreements. When Danny swore and spat angry words after their phone calls she walked on eggshells, tried to reason with him, to calm him down. She would remind him that it was in the best interests of their children to keep a civilised relationship, urging him to forgive and to send conciliatory emails or texts. She often felt like the parent of two bickering children and her efforts were not always well received, with Danny accusing her of taking Susan's side against him.

Lucy had found that she was beginning to enjoy the time she had to herself when Danny was away and she could meet a friend for coffee or just sit alone, reading a book. When he had asked how she felt about him spending time at his old family home with the children, Lucy had given the honest answer that she didn't mind. She thought it was better that he saw them at the house; that way the children were in a familiar setting, and it was easier for them to show him their latest drawings or Lego construction.

The previous week, Susan had told Danny with little notice, that he needed to be at the house for their children while she went out with friends. Danny had done as he was asked and hadn't returned home to Lucy until the early hours of the morning, despite having an early start for work in the morning. He had woken Lucy when he eventually climbed into bed, telling her that he had fallen asleep on the sofa waiting for Susan to return and that he had woken with the television still on and Susan hovering over him, about to kiss his face. When he rejected her advances, Susan had started to cry, begged him to stay, then sank to the floor in front of the door, barring his exit and slurring that she was useless. When he'd asked if she felt fit enough to look after the children, she had been incensed and had lurched angrily at him, shouting and swearing. When he offered to call her mother to come and help, she pushed him out the door, saying that she and the children didn't need him, that the three of them were happier without him. Lucy had listened carefully, only giving an opinion that Susan was going through a stressful time and that she had been drinking. She told Danny that she wasn't concerned about it because she trusted him but she registered a flash of disappointment on his face.

If Danny and Susan argued or if the children got upset when he left, he ran to Lucy's arms, crying and begging her to never leave him. The first time it had happened, she'd thought it quite strange, certain that she had never given him any cause to think that she would end their relationship. She had gently reassured him that he had absolutely nothing to worry about. When it happened more frequently, Lucy began to feel frustrated. She stopped doling out attention and reassurance, sensing that it was being coerced from her. If he had been drinking he wallowed in self-pity, telling her that she was all he had left in the world. It was irritating. She had never been in a relationship where she'd had to work so hard.

When Susan had first found out about their relationship, she had been furious and bitter. She began to be unreasonable or inflexible, effectively denying Danny access to his children. Lucy had sat down with him to discuss their options. She had offered to pay for a family law solicitor to draft some visitation rights, but added that it might antagonise Susan, causing more problems in the long run. She had urged Danny to be patient, to let her be angry and upset, to let the dust settle before taking any official action. Sure enough, Susan had come round and allowed him access again, but when things had looked bleak, Lucy had made it clear to Danny that the children would always come first. She told him that if she was the barrier stopping Danny from being able to be with his children then they would have to split up, even if it broke her heart. She also told him that if Susan was receptive to rekindling their marriage and he wanted that too, he only had to be open and honest with Lucy – she would never stand in the way if there was any hope for them to be a family again.

Before they'd left home for the airport, Lucy had telephoned the garage where Danny's broken-down car was still stuck, waiting for a second-hand part to be sourced. It had been off the road for months, most of the time they had been together, which meant that he used Lucy's car when he went to visit the children, leaving her in an unfamiliar town, away from her friends and family and with no transport. When she tried to broach the subject, Danny brushed it off, reasoning that they were managing with one car between them. Lucy bit her tongue, knowing that he couldn't afford a new part and that he wasn't the one being inconvenienced by his lack of car. In the end she had asked the mechanic to go ahead and order new parts instead, grimacing at the estimated quote of a month's wage. Danny's boss, the agency's commander, had allowed him to use a company car in the interim. He commuted to work in the unmarked car, but didn't want to abuse the privilege by driving it any more than necessary. She rubbed her temples, hoping that by the time they flew home Danny's car would be fixed.

The Rome trip passed quickly in a haze of photographs

snapped at tourist spots, fabulous food and espresso coffees, sipped at street corner cafes, while enjoying a different sort of people-watching.

After another full day of walking round in the heat of the city they had returned to the hotel to cool down, shower and dress before heading out to a final dinner. Danny lay on the bed watching a television news channel while Lucy ran a deep bubble bath, looking forward to a luxurious soak. Danny fell asleep, missing a prearranged time slot to call his children before they went to bed. The constant thrum and vibration of his mobile woke him, but he struggled to locate it, eventually discovering it in the pocket of a discarded jacket. By the time he answered the call, Susan was so angry and shouted so loudly, that Lucy could hear her through the wall as she lay in the bath. Closing her eyes tightly, Lucy held her breath and slid under the bubbles.

Lucy emerged from the bathroom wearing the thick, fluffy, white towelling gown provided by the hotel and her hair wrapped in a towel. Her stomach clenched when she saw Danny's face, he was fizzing with silent rage. Danny hadn't told Susan that he and Lucy were going away on a short holiday, but she had worked out that they were abroad from the tell-tale international dialling tone, which had added to her fury after he had failed to call the children.

Danny paced about the room, giving Lucy details of the call. He stopped abruptly, sat down and pulled on his shoes, tugging frustratedly at the laces, still lost in conversation and restless. Lucy pointed to the towel on her head, and he waited grudgingly for her to dress and dry her hair, muttering under his breath and scrolling through his phone. They had been having such a good time. Not wanting the evening to sour and spoil the end of their trip, Lucy took a deep breath, moving a brush through her hair and trying to work out how she could lift his spirits again.

It was dark by the time they left the hotel. Danny didn't talk as they walked and he kept a couple of steps ahead. Hands thrust deep in his trouser pockets, head down and shoulders hunched, he had the gait of a sulky teenager. As they walked further from the main street, down a narrow, cobbled street, they heard music and laughter. Walking towards the sound, they found a small trattoria full of locals enjoying themselves. The dark interior was dimly lit, but fairy lights strung above the long, brass and marble bar, gave the place a festive air. Lucy's eyes were drawn to the rear of the premises where she could see a brightly lit, tiny kitchen area where a heavily built, grey-haired man, wearing a white apron was engrossed in flipping a skillet of food over the open flame of a stove. She breathed in fresh-smelling bread, garlic and tomato. The small bar area had eight wooden tables crammed inside it. People sat crowded round them on wooden cross-back chairs, huddled in lively conversation and laughter, with glasses, bottles and plates in front of them. Every now and then a harassed-looking waitress delivered a plate of food or tray of drinks. In contrast to the Italian restaurant they had dined in at home this place looked plain and unpretentious, with basic decor and simple, authentic food.

Danny caught the eye of the waitress who bustled over to them and in broken English, told him that there were no tables available, but if they could find space at the bar, they were welcome to wait and she would call them over when one became free. Lucy was relieved to see Danny's face finally relax. He smiled and nodded to the waitress, took Lucy's hand and led her to the bar.

One chair was reserved near the door for an elderly gentleman who was playing a melancholy tune on an accordion with an empty glass on the windowsill next to him. Remnants of beer foam ringed the inside of his glass at different levels, showing where he had managed a few mouthfuls between playing.

Standing at the bar, Danny showed no sign of his earlier foul mood, laughing easily, ordering a glass of wine for Lucy and two bottles of beer – one for himself and another for the accordion player. The evening passed in a blur of good food and copious beers for Danny. He had been reluctant to leave at the end of the night, even when Lucy reminded him that their flight home was early the next morning. Eventually she had ushered him outside and into a taxi.

When Danny was safely tucked up in bed, lying on his back, snoring loudly, Lucy crept about the dimly lit room, fumbling with the fancy coffee machine on the desk before setting it to work. A few minutes later she padded barefoot onto the small balcony, cradling a hot cup of coffee. Enveloped in the dark, with the breath of cool night air on her skin, she sat at a tiny table with headphones on, listening to music and savouring the last of the break.

In the early morning sunshine Lucy got out of bed, showered, dressed, packed for them both and took a fresh coffee onto the balcony. She left Danny to sleep off his beer, waking him thirty minutes before the taxi was due to collect them for the airport. He smelled like a brewery and looked rough. As he got up and staggered, bleary-eyed to the bathroom, Lucy pulled back the sheets to air the bed. She saw a damp patch on the white fitted sheet where Danny had lain. *Oh no!* she thought as she gingerly bent closer to smell it. When Danny emerged from the bathroom, she asked him if he was alright. He looked confused until Lucy gestured towards the damp mattress. His face flushed red from the neck up as he told her that he must have spilled a glass of water. He was so flustered that she let the subject drop, mortified on his behalf and hoping that the damp linen would dry before housekeeping arrived. Danny was quiet and subdued as he swallowed down two paracetamol tablets with a mouthful of coffee. Swaying slightly, he put sunglasses over his bloodshot eyes and they left.

9.

Back at work, Lucy was pleased to find that she had missed nothing and was soon up to speed with Operation Flame. There was still no intelligence to indicate where Lee Aitchison might be hiding out, but Lucy uncovered a flurry of new mobile phone messages, indicating that a drugs delivery was imminent. Scanning the information, Lucy assessed that it would be a reasonable, dealer amount and saw that the courier hailed from Liverpool. Maybe they held a link to Lee's whereabouts? If nothing else, it would bolster their case against the Aitchisons. Lucy called Chris Summers over to her desk and tapped the monitor with a pen.

'See that?' she indicated to the colour-coded, fresh mobile numbers.

'Yes.'

'Now look at this,' she minimised the page and brought up another. 'This is almost a description of the courier.'

Chris read the back-and-forth messages, a slow smile spreading over his face.

There was no doubt in the barely disguised chat that a young woman was on her way to Aberdeen city centre with a package of drugs.

'Okay, folks,' Chris addressed the office. 'We're heading out. Briefing in ten minutes. Lucy, you've got a train to catch. I'll drop you off at Dundee if we can make it there in time.'

After the briefing, Lucy put on her covert harness, pressing the button in her pocket to test it against the earpiece she wore. Gathering kit and preparing to leave, she wondered about the courier, guessing she had racked up a drugs debt that she had no hope of clearing, or was doing it under duress. Either way she had agreed to move £20,000 worth of crack cocaine, gambling on not being caught with somebody else's drugs.

With the rest of the surveillance team on the road and a reception committee of plain clothes officers at the train station ahead, Lucy boarded the train and was soon swaying with the jolts and bumps of the track as she walked through carriages, quietly checking out each of the occupants, looking for the unsuspecting courier.

Finding her mark, Lucy chose a seat with an unobstructed view a couple of rows back. She sat down, casually retrieving a tatty paperback novel and a packet of mints from her handbag while keeping an eye on the young woman. She was in her early twenties, short and almost painfully thin. She wore bobbled, jersey leggings which had gone baggy at the knee. A grubby, white cropped t-shirt was visible under a scruffy, blue denim jacket. Her unwashed limp, home bleached-blonde hair hung in a greasy curtain, covering half of her hollow-cheeked face. She looked on edge, dark circled eyes darting about the carriage. On the scratched, sticky table in front of her sat a well-worn, grey canvas handbag, in which she rooted around, producing half a packet of fruit sweets, handing them to the small child sitting next to her. He was about five years old, wearing a blue, padded jacket which was about two sizes too large for him. Struggling to see over the zipped-up collar, he played with the remains of a Lego figure, absent-mindedly kicking the seat with the back of his training shoes. Looking more closely, Lucy saw that the woman had a child's cartoon character lunchbox on her lap. It looked out of place, its bright cheerful colours contrasted against her drab clothing. She held the plastic carry handle tightly in a small hand, her chipped blue nail polish highlighting the shiny, newness of the box.

Lucy was relieved to see that the child was clean, tidy and apparently content to be in the company of the woman. Watching the two interact, Lucy formed the opinion that the child was not hers, but they obviously knew each other well enough for the boy to be relaxed in her company. There was a distinct lack of contact and rapport between them, which made her think he had been *borrowed* from a friend or a neighbour, deliberately taken along as a decoy.

Turning the page of her book without reading it, Lucy watched the woman squeeze between the table and the boy, the lunchbox still held tight in her hand, leaving the child and her handbag behind. Unsteady on her feet with the movement of the train, the woman dodged past a passenger towards the end of the carriage. Through glass on the automatic doors, Lucy watched her fumble with the door control, then enter the toilet. Carrying out a silent assessment of the remaining carriage occupants, Lucy didn't register any threat to the boy who was busy peeling sticky wrappers from sweets and popping them in his mouth. Nobody else was paying him any attention. Lucy sent a message to the team, letting them know that she had located the courier and that there was a youngster in tow who they would have to factor into their plans.

Five minutes later, the woman returned to her seat with the lunchbox in her hand. She looked sober, but judging by the way she was wriggling around in her seat, Lucy thought it likely that she was *banking*, and that she had visited the toilet to rearrange or insert a drugs package inside herself.

Despite having a lunchbox with her, Lucy saw the nervous young woman attract the attention of an attendant who was wheeling a snack trolley along the carriage. Purchasing a packet of crisps and a box of orange juice, she cast another anxious look around the carriage before settling her gaze back on the box.

The team members who were ahead at the train station were carrying out a sweep, checking it and the surrounding area for any associates of the drug-dealing gang. Lucy heard a crackly, radio message in her earpiece, passing an update to say that the coast was clear. They had expected as much. None of the gang would want to meet the courier at the station, it would be too risky. If she had been spotted or followed by the police, they would be caught with her and there were too many CCTV cameras and circulating British Transport Police officers at the station.

In the carriage, a broken, static voice came over the PA system, announcing that the next stop was ten minutes away and that the train would terminate there. Lucy relayed the announcement to the team and heard a flurry of messages in response as the operatives acknowledged they were in position and waiting.

Turning over a corner at the top of her page to mark her place in the dog-eared paperback, Lucy stowed it in her bag and pulled out her phone. She watched the courier dig out a clean, new-looking mobile phone from her handbag on the table – a burner no doubt. She hastily tapped out a message before replacing the phone and trying unsuccessfully to fit the lunchbox in her handbag.

As the last of the grey, wet countryside slid past dirty train windows, their imminent arrival at the station was heralded by graffitied granite walls, tenement buildings and an increased volume of litter.

As the train slowed, entering the station, a sea of blurred faces passed Lucy's window, all standing on the platform, waiting to board for the next service or to greet arriving friends and family. All around her, passengers reclaimed stowed bags and cases, stood in the aisle, stretching and yawning, or waited impatiently to disembark. As the train ground to a stop, Lucy recognised a couple of colleagues on the platform. A couple more came into view as she got to her feet, bracing her legs against the side of the seats, holding back and smiling to indicate that the courier and the boy could exit before her. The courier moved forward to disembark with her handbag in one hand and lunchbox in the other, looking over her shoulder, checking the boy was right behind her. Lucy naturally followed on, close behind them in the throng of people as they stepped off the train and walked towards the exit, feeling a chill wind run through the draughty station.

As they neared the exit, two plain-clothed officers closed in on the woman and another bent down to speak to the youngster, smiling reassuringly at him. Taking the police officer's hand, the boy skipped happily along with him towards the British Transport Police office on the concourse. As Lucy walked past them, she saw the woman regard the officers with confusion at first, then with a look of resignation as they flashed police ID badges. She sagged and her shoulders dropped as nervous energy left her body. She offered no resistance as the cartoon lunchbox and her handbag were taken from her. Her face looked tired, drawn and even paler than it had on the train. She had no desire to even try to run away from them.

Emerging on to the bustling street, Lucy heard the steady thrum of traffic and cry of seagulls as she walked up to the waiting squad car. Now it would be a waiting game to see what the courier would be prepared to offer up. Lucy bit her lip, hoping the noose was tightening around the Aitchisons.

10.

On a rare run of days off together, Lucy and Danny sat in the well-maintained communal gardens of their flat. Enjoying coffee in the morning sunshine, they debated how to fill the day.

'Nice day for a walk into town and a few drinks,' Danny said, stretching his neck to squint at the sun from behind dark glasses. Lucy studied his face from behind her own shades. Jagged silver and red scar lines down his right cheek were more visible in the bright light. He had explained to Lucy that these were the result of a bicycle crash through the rear window of a parked car, several years ago. Fine lines around his eyes and mouth had settled into crags and his thinning hair was more grey than blonde, but he was still handsome in her eyes, even if he was beginning to look all his years.

She regarded him properly now, seeing a sharpness to his features which she had not noticed before. Despite sitting in the sun with hot coffee in her hand, she shivered, feeling a chill creep up her spine, brought on with the familiar tension of trying to keep him afloat emotionally and financially. She had noticed that alcohol consumption spun the wheel of fortune for his moods, but lately he'd been prone to angry outbursts even when he hadn't been drinking.

She shook her head, a small, involuntary motion, to dismiss gathering doubts, reasoning that he was having a good day today, and things were bound to improve all round once they bought a place of their own. A fresh start. Lucy hoped he'd feel better when he had financial equality, she could tell he felt uncomfortable with the current imbalance, hating to ask her for money but always the one carrying cash when they were out together – an illusion of being 'the great provider'. Seeking a diversion from the pub and wishing to avoid an early drinking session, Lucy suggested they went to the gym. The monthly payments were too steep not to use the place regularly and there had been a hefty joining fee too. They attended so seldom that Lucy had considered cancelling their subscription, but it turned out they were contractually obliged to remain for at least another four months before they could stop paying. Danny agreed and suggested a swim there afterwards.

After their trip to the gym, Danny was in surprisingly good spirits. He prided himself on his trim figure and ability to run further and faster than Lucy. She had never really been a fan of the gym and considered herself lucky to keep a small frame without having to watch what she ate and drank. Running was not her idea of fun, especially on a treadmill in the gym, and unless it was to catch a bus or a train, she considered it pointless. Being moderately active at work was enough for her.

Danny was in such a good mood that Lucy acquiesced when he suggested they go home to park the car, change and walk to their local pub. He was warm towards her and good company, making her feel their future was bright.

An hour later, they walked into the dimly lit local pub. Blinking to adjust her eyes from the bright sunshine outside, noticing a damp, unpleasant smell, Lucy suggested they take their drinks outside. Her eyes fell on a bedraggled-looking mop, in a red plastic bucket, propped against the wall nearest to the gents, a faint smell of vomit mixed with pine-scented cleaning fluid and permeated the air.

'Nah, better in here,' Danny replied, licking lager foam from his lips, nodding towards a couple of stools at the empty bar area. Apart from a small group of elderly men, they were the only customers inside, everyone else preferring the sunny beer garden, with its overgrown weeds and splintered bench seats. Trying to ignore the oppressive smell, Lucy walked straight out of her right shoe as it remained stubbornly behind, gluing itself to the worn linoleum on a dark sticky mess, which might have been chewing gum. She cringed as her foot momentarily contacted the dirty floor before sliding back inside the safety of her shoe. As her eyes adjusted to the low light, Lucy saw the bar surface was not much better, but decided to say nothing, placing her glass on the sticky bar countertop, adding a fresh ring.

After a couple of drinks, Danny suggested they visit his brother in Carlisle. Lucy liked Mike. He and his wife Donna were closer to her age and were good company. Still perched on a bar stool, Danny pulled out his mobile to call Mike, but decided to make a quick call to his children first. Lucy studied a mostly empty, cardboard display of peanut packets hanging behind the bar. She could overhear his son's excited chatter as he proudly told him that they had erected a tent with friends in the back garden and were playing in it. When the conversation became distracted and slow, it was obvious that he wanted to return to the fun. Before long, Susan took the phone, allowing him to whoop and run back to play. Lucy caught snippets of the call where Susan's voice was slightly too loud and shrill. It sounded as if she had been drinking and she made a big deal of letting Danny know that she was hosting a barbecue in *his* old garden, for *his* parents and old friends.

Lucy flinched, hearing her tell Danny that his best friend, Paul, was cooking on the grill – Danny's usual role – and that he was being 'flirty.' This instantly irked Danny. His nostrils flared and his mouth set in a small, tight line. His face grew red as he told her that she was free to flirt with anyone she liked.

'Have a crack at my dad if you like, you slut,' he snapped, in a voice too loud for the quiet pub, before cutting her off, ending the call and slamming his phone on the bar. Lucy felt heat rise from her chest to her face. Her cheeks were burning and she shrank back in her seat. She kept her eyes downcast, afraid to meet his and concerned that he might lash out, she felt he was ready to throw his phone or a glass in rage.

They sat in silence while Lucy concentrated on fishing a loose lemon pip out of her glass, casting her eyes round the gloomy pub to see if they were being watched. Luckily, she saw that the older group were engrossed in arguing over a game of dominoes, or perhaps they knew better than to outwardly show any reaction to the drama at the bar. The bartender remained at the other end of the bar, rattling dirty glasses, rearranging them to fit into a small, undercounter dishwasher. Lucy swallowed nervously, shocked again by Danny's language and the quickness of his temper. She felt uncomfortable and was suddenly conscious of her footwear, regretting her choice of flimsy, slip-on espadrilles. What if she had to run from him? She felt a prickle of discomfort, realising that her train of thought was not normal. She watched his fingers pick at the corner of a soggy beer mat and realised she needed to do something quickly to divert gathering storm clouds of rage.

Downing her drink, she winced as the last contents of

her glass seemed to be neat vodka, the lemonade not properly mixed. Signalling the bartender over, she forced a light tone to her voice and asked for another round. Checking her purse for coins, she asked for change to play the silent jukebox. Despite the bickering domino players, the bar felt as quiet as the grave. With a handful of coins, she walked over to peruse the only jolly-looking thing in the dour place, the brightly lit, electric jukebox fixed to the wall. Slotting home the coins, she pressed buttons until The Jam's distinctive jangling guitar intro for 'That's Entertainment' rang round the pub, breaking the silence. As she selected the next tune, Danny wandered over to join her, drink in his hand, peering over her shoulder and pointing to songs. Lucy chanced a look at him, relieved to see that he looked less angry. His eyes ran along the lists of song titles and bands as he mumbled that he would go outside and call his brother. Lucy gave a tight smile. 'Good idea,' she said. He was visibly calmer now, tapping out a beat with his finger on the glass as he took over the jukebox selection and Lucy slid back to her seat.

Ten minutes later, Danny returned. He perched on the bar stool next to hers and placed an empty pint glass on the bar. He was fidgety, almost hyperactive. He talked quickly, gesticulating as he explained that they would drive down the next morning and spend the night at his brother's place. Looking at his empty glass, she took the opportunity to prevent him ordering another round of drinks by suggesting that they should head home and pack. Maybe collect some takeaway dinner on the way too? He considered this, then nodded in agreement, adding that they could also pick up a bottle of wine.

The next morning, Lucy loaded their overnight bags into the boot of her car. Danny had only managed a couple of paracetamol tablets for breakfast and wore sunglasses despite the overcast day. It had been a struggle to rouse him. He had consumed a bottle of red wine with their takeaway pizza and had then trawled through the kitchen cabinets until he found a bottle of syrupy liqueur, which Lucy had purchased for a recipe she had never got round to making. Not wanting a late night before they drove to Carlisle, Lucy went to bed, leaving him sitting on the sofa watching TV with the last of the liqueur. He had fallen asleep, eventually stumbling through to bed in the early hours of the morning.

By contrast, Lucy felt fresh, and having only had a couple of drinks at the pub, she was happy to drive, letting Danny sleep through the journey, and was looking forward to Sunday lunch with Mike and Donna.

When they finally reached their destination and were parking outside the house, Danny opened his eyes, yawned and started to look more human. The bottle-green t-shirt he wore had a dark patch at the left shoulder, she presumed from where he had drooled on it while asleep. It was amazing how quickly he could fall asleep and how deeply he slept. Like flicking a switch, once he was under, he could sleep through an earthquake. Shaking her head and laughing, she told him to grab the bags while she retrieved flowers and champagne from the footwell behind the driver's seat. Danny looked at the flowers and bottle with confusion on his face.

'We stopped at a service station,' Lucy told him.

'Did we?' he chuckled and walked to the house.

Several hours later, Donna and Lucy sat together, chatting over a glass of wine. Danny and Mike had gone for a walk to the pub, to catch up over a game of darts.

'You make him happy,' Donna told Lucy, smiling.

'I hope so,' Lucy replied, circling the top of her glass with a finger.

Lucy thought she could hear the distinctive creak of the cottage's back door, but when Donna didn't react, she assumed she had been mistaken and it had just been some other sound that the old cottage routinely made.

'When you have the kids to stay, can we come up and see them?' Donna asked.

'Of course. Do you see them often?'

'We're godparents to both of them, but haven't seen them since Christmas Day a couple of years ago.' Donna shrugged. 'Susan and Danny stopped visiting us and we were never invited to their place.'

Lucy tried not to look as surprised as she felt, when Donna told her that Susan considered them to be a 'bad influence' on Danny.

'Why?' asked Lucy

Donna shrugged again and told her she had no idea.

'We didn't discuss it, in case it made things even more awkward with Susan,' Donna said.

'Anyway,' Donna said into her glass, 'I'm so glad Mike and Danny can be together again, so cheers to that.'

They chatted about Donna's work, property prices and which area Danny and Lucy thought they might eventually buy a house. Lucy stifled a yawn as she looked at the wall clock and saw the late hour. Before she could ask what was taking Mike and Danny so long, the back door opened and Mike walked through to the lounge, looking around the room.

'Where's Danny?' he asked.

Seeing their blank faces, he explained that they had been sitting in the pub, having a drink, and chatting about nothing in particular, when Danny had just got up and wandered off. Mike had assumed he had gone to the gents or was outside making a phone call, but when more time passed and he didn't return, he'd gone looking but couldn't find him.

Lucy's eyes widened and her heart began to beat faster, no longer tired, she listened to Mike and Donna try to replay the evening and work out what had happened to Danny. Without speaking, Lucy and Donna stood and went to find shoes and coats. The three of them decided to retrace the route from the cottage to the pub. Lucy felt sick with growing concern as Mike tried out different theories, trying to work out what could have gone wrong and the three of them tumbled out of the cosy cottage into the dark night. There were only a few streetlights in the area, and they were old and dim, making it difficult to see the path at times.

They fanned out, covering the well-trampled path which followed the riverbank, peering into the darkness of shrubs and overgrown hedgerows, looking for Danny, in case he was laid out and in need of assistance. After an hour they had walked the route twice more with no sign of him. The pub was closed but a member of staff eventually answered the door to Mike's persistent knocking, confirming that no one was left inside. She told them that she didn't remember serving Danny and didn't remember seeing him leave. They had no CCTV and none of the other remaining members of staff had seen Danny either.

As they walked back, in the still of the night, calling his name into the countryside, Mike asked if Danny was suffering from depression, being separated from his children, weighing up whether he might have willingly gone into the fast-flowing river.

'No. Definitely not.' Lucy offered, 'He must have had an accident.'

Mike asked if they should call the police to report his disappearance.

'Let's wait until we get back,' Lucy said, her stomach in knots, still hoping desperately they would somehow find him further down the path with a minor injury, maybe a sprained ankle. She tried to calculate how many drinks he had consumed and whether it was possible that he had just decided to sleep it off somewhere outside. Her mind raced as she realised the implications of alerting the police, telling them an off-duty police officer had gone missing. The balloon would go up, bosses would be woken. It might cause him trouble at work if a search party was formed to look for him and it turned out that he'd just got drunk and wandered off. But if he didn't turn up soon, they would have no choice other than to report him as a missing person.

As they walked gloomily back into the bright light of the cottage. Lucy heard music playing on the stereo. The hairs on the back of her neck stood up, as she remembered with certainty that they had not been listening to music that evening. All three entered the lounge, towards the music source, and gasped when they saw Danny sitting in an armchair, muddy shoes resting on a footstool, tumbler of whisky in his hand.

He looked at them and snorted nastily, 'Fools!' Then gave a humourless laugh.

'Where the hell were you?' Mike took only a second, changing from concerned and confused, to incredulous and angry. 'We've been looking all over for you,' he said pointedly.

'I know,' Danny said, turning the whisky tumbler in his hand. 'I've been watching you.'

Mike took an angry step forward but was stopped in his tracks by Donna stepping in front of him, hands up, appealing for peace.

'Leave him. Let's do this in the morning,' she said, taking his hand and steering him towards the stairs.

Lucy was rooted to the spot, mouth hanging open, rapidly blinking, as she fought to understand what was happening. The initial relief she had felt when she saw him safe and in one piece evaporated as she took in the arrogant, nasty person in front of her. Her legs felt weak as she perched on the edge of the sofa, furthest from him and closest to the door. In a shaky voice, she asked him what he was doing.

'I wondered how long it would be until you missed me,' he sneered.

Tears pricked her eyes. She whispered, 'I thought something bad had happened to you.'

'Well, you didn't look very upset and you didn't look very hard,' he said, with glassy eyes on hers.

Lucy's knee started to tremble, nerves working overtime, as he described how he had sneaked back into the cottage and had eavesdropped on her and Donna's *boring* conversation and how he had been disappointed with Lucy's answer to Donna's question of what she saw in him. Lucy's simple reply had been that 'they were good together'. This, Danny told her, was not good enough, and she needed to know that she was not holding all the cards. He could disappear if he wanted, and she should always remember that he would be watching her.

'Always,' he spat.

Then he laughed again and told her, 'I'm trained to stalk people. It's what I do. It's my job.'

Lucy knew she wouldn't sleep that night; his words would run through her addled mind, on repeat. His crazy behaviour had spoiled the newly rekindled relationship with his brother and sister-in-law, and it was lucky they hadn't been asked to leave. She dreaded the resulting awkward breakfast they were yet to have. She wondered if Susan had really been to blame for their last falling out.

11.

Lucy rubbed her gritty eyes. Her head ached from a lack of sleep as she lay motionless in the guest bed at Mike and Donna's cottage. Danny had eventually joined her, hobbling into bed after stumbling and clomping around the bedroom, swearing into the darkness as his toes connected with unfamiliar wooden furniture. Almost as soon as he lay down, he fell into a deep sleep. As the volume of his snoring increased, Lucy told herself to relax, bringing her shoulders up towards her ears, holding, then releasing them, trying to break the tension which had lodged in her muscles again. Her mind was a swirl of jagged thoughts and sleep wouldn't come. Lying perfectly still on her back, Lucy's eyes roved the space where she guessed the ceiling would be, in the coal-black room. Danny's moods had become increasingly bleak lately, but this was another level. She guessed that she must have attended dozens of 'domestic' calls already in her time with the police. Before the police became involved, the situation had often escalated to the point where the victim needed medical attention and injuries could no longer remain hidden. She had dealt with repeat victims, and realised with sickening clarity, that while she had been empathetic and professional, she had never really been able to understand why the victim had not simply walked away from their toxic relationship and the abuser. Although she was acutely aware that it was statistically likely, she had never been able to picture herself or any of her own family and friends being the victims of domestic abuse.

Lucy stared into space, liquid leaking from the corners of her eyes, feeling stupid and miserable. She was not in a domestic-abuse situation, she just needed to get a grip. She was only feeling a bit sorry for herself, and everything always felt magnified and worse late at night. Danny was a different sort of partner, and they were going through a stressful time, she just needed to be strong. But her mind wandered to Danny's remark about overhearing a conversation between herself and Donna. Had Donna asked her what she saw in Danny? She couldn't remember the question being asked, but it seemed a reasonable query, and they had chatted all night, so perhaps she had. She tried to answer the question now but couldn't formulate a response. She made an imaginary list of Danny's pros and cons and came up short for the pros. Then she considered herself, carrying out a sort of 'stock check'. She felt tired, not exclusively from this night; she seemed to be permanently fatigued, relying evermore on coffee and paracetamol to function at her usual speed. She was usually funny, finding any humour in a situation and sharing jokes. Danny had said it was one of the things he liked best about her, but Lucy couldn't remember when she'd last laughed with abandon. She used to have a lightness about her, a difficult-to-define quality, but something optimistic and carefree. She never had any issues that she considered real problems, navigating life easily and having time to help others. Lucy was aware that she had been neglecting friendships and her family, in favour of spending all her spare time with her partner.

Contemplating why she remained with Danny, she supposed that it was because she had an enduring belief that in time to come, the relationship might be everything she wished for, a caring and nurturing place where they shared exciting adventures together. She could see there was also an element of, 'I've made my bed and must lie in it'. The lease agreement for their flat, the joint bank account and gym memberships served to ensnare them in an ever-growing tangle of commitment.

She hadn't told a soul about the punch. Thinking about it now made her hot with shame and embarrassment all over again. She was fortunate enough to have an address book full of caring contacts. Any one of those people, if selected at random and called, would give her support and shelter. Lucy swallowed a lump in her throat, thinking of them now, feeling weak and cowardly. The courage and confidence she used to possess had abandoned her, leaving her unsure and questioning herself. She burned with mortifying humiliation, blaming herself for letting it get so bad, and angry with herself for failing at another relationship. She didn't want to share these feelings with anyone else and most definitely, didn't want anyone at work to find out.

If the cat was let out the bag and there was an investigation, and *if* she was believed, Danny would potentially lose his job, maybe even be sent to prison. What would happen to her? Apart from heaping further embarrassment on herself, Lucy felt certain that her bosses would not be sympathetic of a *messy* domestic situation. She knew that she had done nothing wrong, but she still felt that stigma would stick to her and with it she'd lose her place in the squad. Her stomach roiled at the thought. Speaking up would be to commit career suicide. She'd been in the squad long enough to see colleagues who were regarded by the bosses as *troublesome*, taken aside for the dreaded 'quiet word', resulting in them jumping ship before they were pushed.

She had also seen specialist detectives fall from grace after they had attempted to whistle-blow, having their work questioned and insinuations made that they had some sort of mental illness. Nobody wanted to bring upon themselves an appointment with the 'Nutty Professor', the force's consultant psychiatrist. Better to remain silent, than to be discredited by having your mental health questioned. The agency routinely had their specialist team of housebreakers attend for check-ups, to ensure they weren't going to go off the rails while deployed on a high-risk job.

Danny had told Lucy about a night when he had been out with his team and one of them had become unwell inside their target's home. They'd been rescued by the team who suspected he was having a heart attack. After it was found to be a panic attack, the agency's commander had been less than sympathetic, and a move from the department swiftly followed.

Danny was well liked by the commander who confided in him, treating him as a peer, despite the large gap between their ranks, discussing sensitive information and belittling Danny's supervisors. The two always seemed to be in cahoots when Lucy saw them together. His affair with a junior colleague was one of the worst kept secrets in the agency. Lucy recalled what Roddy had said on the matter when it had been discussed with other office gossip.

'Well, it seems we were all wrong. There we were, thinking she was completely useless, but there's obviously something she's good at.'

Lucy might have issues to sort in her home life, but she would be damned if she would be judged by the chauvinistic executive. The commander would certainly take Danny's side over hers if anything came to light, she was sure of that.

The long night and lack of sleep was making her head feel like it was full of cotton wool and her thoughts became foggy. Maybe it was her fault. Maybe she brought out the worst in Danny, not the best, causing him to over drink and to overreact. She chewed her lip, contemplating how he had seemed before they got together – apparently sane and well liked by his colleagues. She realised that he had never mentioned any friends outside the job, apart from Paul, who had been an old neighbour. He occasionally spoke about a group of football fans, acquaintances he used to meet on a match day, with whom he would have a drink and go to watch the game, but that was all. No other hobbies or friends that she was aware of.

Eventually, after what felt like an extraordinarily long night, the dawn's weak, grey light filtered through, showing a floral pattern on the bedroom curtains. In the dingy light, Lucy saw her already packed bag and doubted there would be any fond farewells before they left.

When she heard floorboards creaking, soft footsteps on the landing and water flowing through pipes, Lucy got up and dressed. She went downstairs to find Donna already sitting at the kitchen table, looking tired and strained, cradling a steaming mug.

'Want some? Help yourself,' she said gesturing her mug towards a jug of filter coffee.

'Thanks,' Lucy said, smiling weakly. 'I'm sorry,' she offered.

'You don't have anything to apologise for,' Donna told her. 'I thought he'd changed, but it seems not.' Donna sounded deflated, not angry.

Lucy sat down at the table and sighed. 'I'm shattered,' she admitted. 'He's got me on tenterhooks.' As she said it aloud, she knew the relationship couldn't continue. Donna's eyes met Lucy's and she patted her arm, shaking her head sadly.

Two hours later, Lucy drove Danny towards home. He hadn't bothered with his sunglasses and his eyes looked bloodshot and baggy. He seemed thoroughly miserable. Feeling sorry for him and, despite herself, Lucy suggested he try to sleep on the way home so that he could make the most of an afternoon with his children.

'I'll need to borrow your car,' he said. Her grip on the steering wheel tightened at the thought of being stuck at the flat again. She said nothing, too tired to go through it all. His broken-down car, the angry ex-wife and their finances. She hadn't brought up the subject of his behaviour from the night before. All he'd offered was to complain that his head was 'banging', and that he thought he must have had too much to drink. Lucy gritted her teeth, there was no point in upsetting him before he went to spend time with the children.

Danny placed his hand on top of hers as it rested on the gearstick, turning his face to look at her, as she stared at the road ahead. She inhaled, maybe this was the apology she'd been waiting for?

'Marry me?' he said earnestly.

'What?' she replied, buying time, her chest tightening, concentrating on the road ahead and not quite believing what she was hearing.

'Let's not mess about,' Danny said. 'I want us to have family together, the sooner the better. So let's get married'.

'Danny,' Lucy reasoned, 'you're already married. We've talked about this.' She was exasperated but kept her response as soft as she could, trying not to give him grounds for an argument or to be nasty to her. Marrying him was absolutely the last thing she wanted to do, but she instinctively knew better than to voice the thought. Trying to placate him, she added, 'There's no rush. We already have family to look after. Maybe we don't need kids of our own.'

Danny inhaled noisily, his voice found a nasal, sharper edge as he told her, 'Don't leave me. If you leave me, I've got nothing. Nothing. I've given up my whole life for you.'

Lucy pushed her left foot against the footwell, steadying her leg to prevent it from shaking. She sensed that she was in danger and feared that he might lash out at her while she was driving, to grab the handbrake or do something equally reckless. She wondered what exactly he believed he had given up for her, but did not say it. Seeking a diversion, she steered the conversation to the afternoon ahead and to his children, suggesting that he take them swimming, or that they go to the cinema.

'Can't,' said Danny, looking dead ahead, his face emotionless. 'Susan's going out with her mates and I've got to babysit'.

'But surely the three of you could still go into town, while Susan's out?' Lucy countered.

'No. She told me we need to stay in.'

'Okay.' Lucy didn't understand the logic, but she said no more on the subject.

Not bothering to find a parking space, Lucy stopped the car outside their flat, getting out and removing overnight bags from the boot, while Danny jumped in the driver's seat. Watching her car pull away, Lucy felt heavy with fatigue as she trudged towards the front door.

Lucy busied herself cleaning the already clean flat and sorting laundry. Too tired to go for a walk or to read, she selected calming background music and sank into a warm bath. The rhythmic vibration of her phone on the edge of the basin brought her back to the present. Splashing water on the floor, she scrambled for a towel to dry her hand before grabbing the phone as it slid into the empty basin, still vibrating urgently with an incoming call. She saw that the caller ID was the garage where Danny's car was being repaired. Desperate not to miss the call, hoping for good news, she answered with a bright, 'Hello?'

The dour mechanic told her that the car was finally repaired and ready to go.

'I didn't think you'd be open today,' Lucy said.

'Aye, I wouldn't normally be here, but I'm trying to catch up.'

Lucy told him she'd do her best to get round for it before he locked up for the day. Thanking him, she hung up, got out the bath and dried quickly. Pulling on fresh clothes she calculated that if Danny picked her up as soon as he got back from visiting the children, they would have enough time to get to the garage and collect his car. Danny had said that he would pick up a takeaway dinner for them on his way home, but Lucy reckoned they would need to go to the garage first to catch it before closing. She wanted it back without any further delay. At last, she would be able to make plans to catch up with her friends on the days when he was away with the children. She realised that she was still planning a future with him, it would all work out, she thought. The car was a good omen.

Lucy sent a text to Danny asking him to call her urgently. When she had not received the expected call back and the message had not been read, she guessed that he had the phone on silent mode, tucked away in a pocket while he played with the kids. Lucy dialled the number, reasoning that persistent vibration might attract his attention. When it rang out, Lucy wasn't concerned – she would try again later. She smiled at the prospect of finally collecting his old car, absent-mindedly planning what they would replace it with, now that it was fit to be traded in for something better.

As she stood at the kitchen sink, filling the kettle, Lucy's gaze fell on the memo board clinging to the side of their fridge. Included in a random list of numbers and information was Danny's old address with the landline number. Lucy pulled out her mobile and switched on the kettle while she dialled.

After only a few rings her call was answered by a child. Taken by surprise, Lucy realised she was talking to Danny's son. She had not expected the 7-year-old to answer the phone and she had hoped for a better introduction, so she simply asked, 'Can I please speak to your dad?'

The little voice was barely audible over a children's cartoon playing in the background, but she distinctly heard him say, 'He's upstairs. I'm not supposed to go up. They're having a sleep.'

Had he made a mistake? What exactly did he mean by 'they're'?

'Who's sleeping?' she gently probed.

'My mummy and my daddy,' came the reply she felt that she had already known.

Lucy's head swam, she felt dizzy and her legs turned to jelly as she understood exactly what it meant. Not ready to believe it, she pulled a chair over and sat down with a heavy heart.

'Are you sure your mummy's there?' Lucy enquired, needing to be certain of the facts.

'Yes, silly! She gave us sweeties and told us to be good and quiet because they were very sleepy,' the childish voice assured her.

'Okay, thank you,' Lucy managed and ended the call with her ears ringing, feeling like she was having an out-of-body experience.

'What the hell?' she asked herself, out loud, alone in her kitchen. Lucy had never considered that Danny might lie to her about his relationship with Susan. In her presence, he had apparently struggled to be civil towards her, forcing himself to do so for the sake of maintaining a relationship with their children. She had never doubted him, had never considered that he might lie to her or be unfaithful to her with anyone, far less with Susan. She stopped wringing her hands and they balled into fists in her lap, as she recalled occasions when he had made her feel awkward and guilty, going on about the long hours she had been working, asking who she had been working with; the insinuations that every male colleague and acquaintance wanted to be with her. Lucy had shrugged it off, telling herself it just meant that he loved her. She had consistently reassured him that she only had eyes for him and that she would never leave him. It struck her that she had begun to deliberately refrain from mentioning certain male colleagues to him, conscious of his jealousy and mistrust, not wanting to upset or provoke him.

Lucy's heart thumped with hurt and injustice as she pulled on her training shoes, suddenly desperate for fresh air and to be outside. She grabbed her bag and coat, banging the door closed behind her. Adrenaline coursed through her, chasing away tiredness and making her feel sick. She strode away from the flat, away from his clothes and possessions.

As she walked briskly on, the physical effort disguised her heavy breathing and her mind cleared. A spell had been broken, the fog of fear vanished and she could finally think straight. She would never again have to squash herself just to sustain his fragile ego. The relationship was over. There was no difficult decision to be made. It was done, but she still had to face him.

12.

After an hour of walking, Lucy felt calmer and more composed. She was betrayed but relieved. He had handed her a key to the cage of their relationship. Her feet had taken her to the local cinema and she purchased a ticket for the next film, not even bothering to ask what was being shown. Feeling parched, she walked towards the snacks counter, smelling popcorn and hotdogs. Her stomach growled in response. She had no appetite but paid for a hot dog and a Coke anyway, hoping it might give her energy for the heart-to-heart ahead. Her stomach twisted at the thought. She hoped the film might distract her enough to suspend reality. Lucy found her seat and gulped cold cola, gratified to see the opening credits were for a thriller, not a rom-com. She was definitely not in the mood for anything involving romance.

Before the film had even started, Lucy's mobile phone began to vibrate in the bag at her feet. Although she had switched off the ringer, the regular pulsing of the phone caused the contents of her bag to jiggle and was distracting. Sighing, she placed the uneaten hot dog on the floor, a safe distance from her feet, picked up her bag and switched the phone off. The screen briefly showed a tally of missed calls, text messages and voicemails which she assumed would be from Danny. She didn't check, having no interest in what he might have to say. She imagined he would have been told by now that *someone* had called the house, asking to speak to him. He was bound to have joined the dots, realising that he had been rumbled.

Lucy fidgeted but forced herself to remain seated and to keep the phone switched off. Hidden in the dark cave of the auditorium, she allowed tears to spill unchecked down her face as the handful of other cinema goers all looked ahead, enchanted by the big screen. As the film ended, and before the lights came on, Lucy got to her feet and left the cinema, disposing of the uneaten hotdog and empty paper cup as she left. Blinking in the brightly lit foyer, she checked her watch, and with a heavy heart, headed for home.

As soon as Lucy walked through the front door of the flat, she saw Danny pacing about the hallway. One hand was raking through his hair as the other worked his mobile phone. She had never seen him look so dishevelled and uncertain before. Danny looked up, having heard Lucy enter the flat and quickly shoved his phone into the pocket of a navy-blue hooded sweatshirt. Distractedly, she noticed that it looked new and that she had never seen it before. It made her wonder if he had a whole wardrobe of other clothes at Susan's house. She held tightly to her bag to disguise her shaking hands and walked past him, giving him a wide berth, denying him contact as he reached out. Keeping her coat on, she sat down, perching at the far end of the sofa. She stared at the carpet in front of her feet and waited for him to start the conversation, expecting an apology or half-hearted excuse of some kind. Her jaw slackened when he asked instead, 'What the hell did you think you were doing, phoning the house?'

She raised her eyes, staring at him as he stared at the ceiling; his face flushed and his mouth an angry gash. She blinked rapidly, trying to process the words as he carried on, telling her that under no circumstances was she ever to call the house again. Not 'Susan's house', she heard; it was *the* house. She didn't fill the empty air when he had finished talking, instead she hugged her bag to her chest as he began to pace again. After a long pause, she told him evenly, 'You gave me the number. I only called it because I couldn't reach you on your mobile and I was trying to arrange the collection of your car from the garage.'

Her measured words halted him. He rocked back and forth on his heels, hands jammed in his pockets, gazing at the floor. Lucy's heartbeat filled the silence in the room until Danny eventually blurted the cliché she had been waiting for. The last line of his self-defence, 'It wasn't what you think.'

The truth was written all over his guilty face and he knew she could see it. He felt the shift, could see that she would not compete for his affection, that she had already written him off. In a last attempt to thaw her, he dropped to his knees, grabbing at her hands, wheedling. 'We were only in the bedroom to talk.'

Lucy gently pulled her hands free, dug her mobile from the bottom of her bag and played a voicemail message on speakerphone. Susan's voice, pinched and maniacal, filled the room. Laughing mirthlessly, she announced that Lucy was an idiot and asked how it felt to be cheated on. Danny made a grab for the phone, but Lucy moved it out of reach as Susan said that she and Danny had just had the best sex ever. Danny shrank away from the phone, his face crumpled. Unable to conjure a suitable lie, he began noisy, tearless crying. Lucy got to her feet, dodging Danny's hands as they reached for her ankles.

Ignoring desperate pleas, Lucy told him, 'I would never stand between you and your family, you know that.'

'No! I don't want her. I want you. Don't say we're finished,' Danny begged, wiping strings of saliva onto the sleeve of his hoodie. Lucy stood straighter, looked down at him and wondered what she had ever seen in him. She had sat in the cinema steeling herself, expecting to find it hard to let him go, but now felt nothing.

'Phone your wife,' Lucy told him, watching him flinch at her use of the word 'wife'. 'She's been ringing my number all evening. Tell her to stop contacting me. She's welcome to you, but leave me out of it.'

Danny curled into a ball on the carpet as Lucy walked out the room.

Lucy gathered the items she thought would be most important to Danny, picking up his passport and other documents and placed them in his gym bag, leaving it open on the bed – an invitation for him to continue packing. She then began to stow some of her clothes, stuffing a charging cable and wash bag in a large black rucksack, as Danny watched miserably on from the doorway.

'I'm going to stay away tonight. That'll give you time to pack up your things and go. You can take your company car and move into Susan's,' Lucy said, still packing her own bag.

Danny shuffled off towards the kitchen. Lucy could hear his phone already ringing and hoped it would be Susan, urging him to return. She could hear him silence the call and then heard a loud thunk, as his phone landed on the floor, thrown in a temper tantrum of defeat. Lucy hurried to finish collecting her things, the hairs on the back of her neck stamding to attention at his worsening mood. Without looking back, she left the flat, tossing the rucksack into the boot of her car. Suddenly weary, she stood shivering in the chill night air. She would book into a hotel tonight and tomorrow she would go to work as usual. There was no need to disturb any of her family or friends this evening, seeking a bed for the night. He would be gone by the time she returned home from work the next day and then she would spend the evening cleaning the flat from top to bottom, removing every trace of him.

13.

Driving to work the next morning, from the cheap and not very cheerful hotel where she had stayed the night, Lucy's eyes felt puffy and a glance in the rear-view mirror showed they looked as bad as they felt. She would say she was suffering from seasonal allergies if any of her colleagues asked, although she doubted anyone would notice. She kept her head down, grateful to suspend her home-life worries by keeping busy at work.

As she sat at her desk, staring at a blank computer screen, Lucy's phone vibrated. She held it up and saw a series of texts from Danny. He had sent several more overnight, disturbing her regularly until she had eventually switched it off. Aware of Roddy's eyes on her, she swiftly tucked it away in her trouser pocket. Waiting for the morning briefing to start, Lucy unlocked her top desk drawer, to retrieve an assortment of documents relating to Operation Flame. As she flicked through the most recent pages of Ralph Aitchison's mobile phone calls and messages, her own mobile phone began to buzz again in her pocket.

'Jesus.' said Roddy, between slurps of his coffee, 'Are you dealing now?' A handful of their colleagues chuckled as Lucy willed her face not to turn beetroot. Before she had to endure any more banter, Inchy walked into their office and lead them through a roundup of their ongoing operations. Taking her turn, Lucy gave the team what little news she had. Drugs had been recovered from the courier on the train, but she had remained resolutely mute when interviewed about them. The mobile phone she had been carrying when she was arrested had been examined and found to have a call history linking it to one of Lee Aitchison's underlings. There were no notable updates from the murder enquiry and Lee was still absent.

'Right,' said Inchy, as he scribbled some notes in his daybook. Turning to Lucy, he told her, 'I've got a wee job for your team.'

Lucy, Chris and the rest of their group, gathered in Inchy's office for details after he had finished the briefing.

'I need you to head to Tayside,' he told them, checking his notes. 'There's not enough happening with the Aitchisons right now to keep you here on stand-by. Tayside have requested assistance with a murder enquiry and you're going to help them for a couple of days. I did warn them that you might have to leave the plot at short notice if we get a lead on Operation Flame. It'll be good practice for you.' He smiled sarcastically, then read out the name of the Crime Scene Manager, reeling off a phone number before waving his hand to dismiss them.

Huddled in Chris's smaller office with the rest of her team, Lucy watched him dial the number on his desk phone.

'Hello, mate. It's Chris here, from the squad. I've been asked to give you a bell about a surveillance deployment on a murder.' He smiled, 'Don't swear, I've got the team with me and you're on speakerphone.'

'Alright, Chris? Haven't seen you for a while. I won't say anything about your football team if I've got an audience,' he chuckled. 'Aye, bit of a strange one here. I'm still at the locus. The victim's a twenty-one-year-old lassie.'

He stood in the narrow hallway of her flat, wearing a white paper suit with blue plastic overshoes, a mask hung under his chin while he spoke on the phone. At his feet was a dark stain on the light grey carpet, blood drying where the victim had lain. His eyes traced blood spots up the wall and onto the ceiling above, then he peered through the sparsely furnished flat.

'Haven't got a motive yet. She had only moved in to the flat a couple months ago and according to her sister she didn't have friends in the area yet. She mentioned a *weird* neighbour, but to be honest there's a few of them here. Looks like a handbag and a purse have been stolen. Our most likely suspect is a young woman who lives in the same building. She's got previous for fraud and petty assault, but nothing like this. I'm hoping we might get DNA from the locus, but that takes time, as you know. In the meantime, I want to know where she is so that we can make the arrest as soon as there's enough physical evidence. I'd also like to know what she gets up to between now and then.'

'Okay, mate. I'll give you time to get back to your office and call you again for the details. We'll head down now.' Chris rang off, looked at the team, shrugged and told them, 'The boss reckons we'll be on this for a couple of days, so pack your bags and phone home now if you need to tell your other halves not to bother making your dinner. Everyone up for this?'

Lucy was in no rush to go back to the empty flat and start deep cleaning to remove all traces of her cheating ex-partner. An interesting case and long hours would be a welcome distraction and prevent her from wallowing in self-pity. It would also help her ignore the persistent, unanswered calls and texts she was receiving from Danny. Every time a new message rolled across the screen of her phone, her heart sank. She had stopped opening them when it became obvious that they were all variations on a miserable theme; of how he missed her and that he wanted them to get back together.

As Lucy juggled heavy kit, her overnight bag and a set of car keys, she heard her phone ping with a new message. She thought she had set it to silent mode, but it must have been knocked back into life while she was shifting equipment. Sighing, she looked at the screen as she silenced it again, expecting to see yet another message from Danny, but was pleasantly surprised to see the sender was 'Mum'.

Putting down heavy bags, she opened the message and read, *The flowers are absolutely beautiful XX*. An array of floral and heart emojis followed. Confused, Lucy made a quick call, not having enough time for a back-and-forth question session and emoji-fest. Her mother answered on the second ring, immediately thanking her for the 'massive' floral arrangement which had just been delivered.

'I didn't send them,' Lucy told her. 'Is there a card and what does it say?'

'Well, they won't be from your brother, and the card says, *To the best mum in the world XXX*.'

'No name?' Lucy asked her mum to send a text with the name of the florist, saying that she would sort it out later. Reassuring her that she could keep the flowers in any case, Lucy said that if they had been sent to the wrong address, as she suspected, the florist would need to know so that a replacement arrangement could be dispatched to the correct recipient. Lucy would pay for them, rather than disappoint her mother by having them taken away. Mulling it over, she wrangled kit and bags into the car and headed to Dundee to await further instruction.

At the end of another long day, Lucy and a couple of her colleagues queued at the reception desk of a faceless, modern hotel, waiting to check in. It had been smooth sailing so far. They had quickly found the suspect, followed her around the city and left her when she settled into the temporary accommodation she had been allocated until the SOCO team were finished in her building. Checking her watch, Lucy calculated that they should have just enough time to dump bags in their rooms and make it into town for a hot meal before every kitchen closed for the night. Chris Summers walked into the hotel foyer, reading his phone. Reaching reception, he looked up to greet the others.

'Anybody hungry?' he asked. A resounding positive reply was followed with nominations for different restaurants they had seen on the way to the hotel. After a debate, they settled on an Indian restaurant, just as Lucy had known they would from the start. They always did. She also knew that they would all follow a familiar pattern of ordering too much food and overeating. Chris went back outside to make a call, returning to let them know that he had booked them a table, 'Just get yourselves sorted as quickly as you can and I'll meet you there.'

A little later, Lucy slid into a booth at the appointed restaurant. She was only the second of the team to arrive, but already seven pints of lager sat waiting, causing patches of condensation to leach on the red tablecloth. Inhaling warm, spicy air, Lucy shrugged off her jacket, reached for a glass, and thanked her colleague with a nod, taking a draught of lager. Her stomach rumbled in anticipation as she looked over the menu, mentally making her choice while helping herself to a popadom. Now she thought about it, she realised this would be the first hot meal she had eaten in a couple of days, and she was ravenous.

Soon they were all congregated around the table, chatter and laughter replaced by concentrated eating and drinking. They had an early start in the morning, and Lucy could already feel the relaxing effects of a beer buzz. With heavy eyes and a satisfyingly full stomach, she asked the attentive waiter for coffee, leaving the rest of the crew to another round of lager. She didn't expect the coffee to keep her awake, in fact, she could hardly wait to lie down and close her eyes. When the pull of a comfortable bed became too hard to resist, she made her excuses, preparing to leave the table. Her departure was met with groans and appeals to stay for one more drink. She could see that for the rest of them, the evening was just beginning. There was a certain kind of bonding which happened when they worked away from home, and it would be slightly broken when she left. There was an unspoken connection which strengthened, uniting them as a team, whenever they shared a few drinks. The same old war stories and well-worn jokes were trotted out, Lucy enjoyed the feeling of camaraderie and belonging it brought.

Lucy yawned, dead-beat, and decided that she was definitely going, declining the proffered 'one for the road'. When Roddy jokingly asked her if she wanted company, she played along with the game by rolling her eyes. She left her share of the bill on the table and bid goodnight to the happy group.

Walking back to the hotel, Lucy checked her phone. Another seven text messages, all from Danny, and all would go unanswered, just like the previous lot. He was persistent, she gave him that. Just seeing his name on the screen of her phone had burst the small bubble of contentment she had felt, dropping her back into a well of sadness. Feeling the loss like a stone in her stomach, she didn't want to be alone in an unfamiliar hotel room, in a strange city. She hurried back, ran a comforting bath and made a call.

Lucy's best friend, Fiona Cunningham, picked up on the first ring, just as Lucy had fully opened the cold tap to balance the water temperature.

'Bloody hell! Where are you?' her friend asked. 'White-water rafting?'

Lucy laughed, placing her phone carefully on the closed toilet lid, on loudspeaker, keeping it safely away from the water as she climbed in. She chatted easily with her friend, apologising for not being in touch sooner, and then again for not being able to meet her for a coffee the next day. Fiona understood that Lucy's job took up most of her time, and frequently got in the way of their plans – she was in a similar position herself. They had met years ago, while going through basic training together at Tulliallan Police College and had been firm friends ever since.

Lucy's mind had drifted, and she realised that she must have missed some of what Fiona had said. There was a pause in the conversation, where Fiona had obviously asked her a question and was waiting for a response. Lucy had to ask her to repeat herself.

'I said, can Danny spare you for a few days? We could do with a proper catch-up or maybe even a weekend away?'

Lucy's heart felt heavy again at the mention of his name. She was too sad and too tired to go through it all with Fiona tonight. She didn't trust herself to speak without crying again, and she was sick of crying. She decided to wait until they met for a proper catch up to fill her in on the whole story. Agreeing to a weekend away with her friend, Lucy thought there would be plenty of time to discuss it then.

'Excellent!' Fiona enthused. 'It's brand new and we'll be guinea-pig tourists, the first to try it.'

Lucy realised she'd missed quite a bit of the conversation, as she pieced together that Fiona's aunt had expanded her bed and breakfast business on the island of Tiree, and now had a self-catering, wooden pod in her garden. It sounded fantastic, just what she needed: good company in a beautiful location. Ending the call, Lucy got out of the bath, cursing softly as she realised that she'd completely forgotten to contact the florist about the arrangement that her mother had received. She resolved to make a call in the morning and get to the bottom of it. She set an alarm and plugged her phone in to charge, settling into bed.

Early the next morning, Lucy was awoken by the vibration of her mobile phone at the bedside. She opened her eyes, trying and failing to focus her blurry vision on the screen, answering the call without thinking. 'Hello?'

She heard Danny's voice, gravelly and flat: 'I didn't expect you to pick up.'

Instantly Lucy was wide awake, unplugging the phone from its charging cable and sitting up in bed. Shaking off sleepy confusion, she remembered that she was in a hotel, working away from home.

'Where are you?' Danny continued, not waiting for a response. 'I sat outside the flat for most of the night, but you didn't come home. You're not at your parents' house either.'

A chill ran through Lucy's veins as she remembered the flowers delivered to her mother.

'That was you,' she stammered. 'You sent flowers to my mum.'

Danny laughed. 'Your mum's nice. I think we should visit her soon. I'd like to be properly introduced.'

Lucy's throat constricted and went so dry that she couldn't make any sound as she digested the information. He hadn't just sent flowers, he had delivered them. She had never told him exactly where her parents lived. She had mentioned the small village she'd grown up in and had spoken in general terms about the family house where they still lived, but she was certain that she had never given the address. She had never taken him to visit and they hadn't been to the flat yet. Her heart hammered. She grasped the phone tightly and moved it away from her, staring at it warily, as if Danny could see through it. Bringing it back to her ear, Lucy's voice wobbled as she told him, 'Stay away from my family.'

'Anyway, I've got to go now,' he said. 'I hope you enjoyed your Indian meal last night.' Feeling sick, she cancelled the call and ran to the bathroom, retching as she reached the toilet. She wiped her mouth with the back of her hand, tasting curry from the previous evening's meal, and sat on the edge of the bath. Her right knee bounced up and down uncontrollably with nervous tension. The shrill tone of her phone rang out in the bedroom, causing her to gasp, until she recognised it was the alarm and forced herself to calm down. Still feeling shaky, struggling to comprehend why Danny would go to her parents' home address, she brushed her teeth twice, took a shower, packed and got ready for work.

Lucy met the rest of her team in the basement garage of the hotel. There were a few bloodshot eyes and plenty of yawns to suggest a late night. Chris handed round paper cups of coffee which were gratefully received as he gave them line-up pairings and let them know the objective for the day. He'd received an update from the murder SIO that the motive had been established as robbery. Lucy was saddened to think that the suspect had snuffed out the life of her neighbour for a small sum of money.

'Financial,' Chris went on. 'Mark cash or cards, and a handbag has been confirmed as missing from the locus. Pass a full description of her clothing and any handbag the subject has in her possession.'

Her day already off to a bad start, Lucy was paired with Roddy. At least he looked a bit livelier now that the coffee was kicking in.

'You and me, doll,' he told her, handing the car keys over.

'Nope,' Chris told Roddy. 'Lucy's on foot; you're driving. Everywhere the subject goes, we go. If she goes to a toilet, I need her to be followed. We need to stay close and we don't want to give her the opportunity to dispose of anything.'

Two hours later, Lucy was seated a couple of rows behind the subject, who was travelling by bus towards the city centre. She was a remarkably unremarkable young woman, with mousy, shoulder-length hair and bitten fingernails. Lucy sent a series of coded clicks through her covert, body-worn radio set. She listened to Roddy through her earpiece, responding to his questions with more clicks. Their subject was in possession of a black handbag with a shoulder strap, which matched the description of the murder victim's missing one. So far so good.

Alighting from the bus, Lucy followed the subject, and joined a handful of people entering a shopping mall. Keeping a discreet distance, Lucy followed her into a shop and browsed a selection of women's clothing. She picked up a navy-coloured linen top and followed the subject to queue at the checkout. Now directly behind the subject, she watched as the woman took out a bank card from an oversized blue purse, as payment for a pair of jeans and chatted easily with the cashier. With her purchase in a carrier bag, the suspect walked away from the till, smiling happily. Lucy placed the linen top on the counter and passed a message to the team, alerting them that the subject was leaving the shop by another exit. Lucy marked the suspect's transaction with her own purchase, smiled politely at the cashier and left with her new top. She heard one of her colleagues through her earpiece, giving an update that the subject had left the shop and was walking away. The team worked together seamlessly, gathering and passing information until the suspect returned to her digs and Chris's voice came over the radio asking them to stand down. Lucy made her way to the designated rendezvous point, meeting the rest of the team in a nearby park.

They fuelled up on more coffee from a kiosk and stood to debrief. Chris told them that the financial transaction had already yielded evidence that the victim's bank card had been used to pay for the jeans. Lucy's mind wandered and she realised that she had never seen a real murderer act like they were portrayed in books and on screens. The ones she had dealt with were mundane, ordinary, not mask-wearing monsters. It was chilling how very average they seemed.

The team hung about, returning to the kiosk for burgers and bacon rolls, waiting for instruction and their next deployment. Roddy tried and failed to miss his shoes with debris falling from the overstuffed burger he was eating. Turning to Lucy, he said with a mouthful of food, 'Your Danny is a great lad.'

Lucy felt her skin prickle at the mention of his name, but she tried to keep poker faced. 'Hmmm?' she replied, glad to have a cup of coffee in front of her face.

'Yeah, he was on the phone to me last night. Said you two are house-hunting and you might even end up living near me.'

Lucy coughed, choking as coffee went down the wrong way. No wonder Danny had known where she'd been, and what she'd eaten for dinner last night. She knew that Danny and Roddy had recently attended the same training course, but Danny had only ever spoken about Roddy being a clown, there was no friendship there. Roddy looked up to him though, and would no doubt welcome any opportunity to ingratiate himself, hoping it might lead to a job in his team. Lucy did not set him straight about her relationship with Danny. It was none of his business and she didn't want Roddy gossiping about her. She made a mental note to be wary of what she said at work. She turned away from Roddy, feeling vulnerable that Danny had managed so easily to get information about her from him. She crushed the coffee cup. House-hunting? He must have said it knowing that Roddy would report straight back to her. Why? Just to unsettle her? Or to tell her that he didn't consider the relationship over? She kicked at the ground with the toe of her shoe. He was certainly bold to be pestering her with calls and texts and by paying a creepy visit to her parents. He had been with her long enough to know that she liked to keep her private life to herself, and that she wouldn't report him to the 'real' police. Lucy's chest tightened, she needed to be on her guard and was glad to be going away for the weekend with Fiona. The longer she spent from the flat, the better. Especially if he was calling round and keeping watch.

Chris wandered back towards them and handed over a ticket. Lucy read the printed information. 'A gig?'

'The subject is going to a concert tonight and so are we.'

'I like them,' Lucy said. The band was an older one. They'd had success with a couple of singles in the charts, back in the day.

'Worse gigs to have,' Roddy said, draining the last of his coffee. 'At least you're getting to see them. I'll just be the chauffeur'.

That evening Lucy wore her new linen top to the gig. Standing inside the venue, leaning against a wall, she watched the suspect dance energetically, shouting out the lyrics. As the song ended, Lucy passed a message to the team, letting them know their subject was heading towards the exit. The gig was still underway, so it looked likely that she was going out for a smoke during one of the quieter songs. Five minutes later, the subject unknowingly asked one of Lucy's team for a light. Cupping her hands round the flame, she puffed on her cigarette.

'This is the life,' she said, exhaling smoke and smiling. Lucy listened to updates being passed thick and fast. Uniformed officers were approaching, Lucy stood in the doorway, watching the suspect's face fall as they stepped in front of her. She hoped that when the time came, the Aitchisons' arrests were as straightforward.

14.

Back at her flat, Lucy finished vacuuming the hallway carpet. The whole place had been cleaned from top to bottom. She had bagged the few remaining items and clothing belonging to Danny and had planned to dump it on Susan's doorstep, but she was eager to pack for her weekend away and didn't want to face bumping into her or Danny. Instead, she had settled for 'out of sight, out of mind' locking the bags in a communal storage cupboard until she got back and plucked up the courage to drop them off. She had given him plenty of time to clear his things out, she wondered if it had been a deliberate decision by him to leave some things, a possible excuse for him to return.

Locking the storage door, she went back inside the flat. It smelled of fabric softener and every surface shone. She smoothed new bedlinen with satisfaction. A fresh start. With music playing softly, Lucy started to pack a bag for her weekend away with Fiona.

Danny had posted his keys through the letter box, as she had asked him to do, but he could have had spares cut and she had the distinct impression that he had been back while she was away working. He had told her that he had been sitting in his car, outside the flat when she was away with work, but he was a liar and could have easily entered when sure she was absent. She shivered at the thought, wishing she was closer to the end of the rental agreement. There seemed little point in changing the locks for such a short time and since his job was breaking into properties for the police, it would give her no peace of mind. She'd just be wary. Part of the reason for cleaning the flat so thoroughly was that she would be able to see if anyone had been there while she was out. She had already begun to look for a new, permanent place to stay, somewhere closer to her family. She was still stung and saddened by the end of the relationship, but she was beginning to feel a little brighter without his presence. He was still sending messages but at least he had stopped calling now. There had been no more mysterious visits to her parents and no sign of him hanging around outside the flat. Still, she felt uneasy. She kept the blinds of the ground-floor flat firmly closed, angled so that even if someone had their face pressed against the windows, they wouldn't be able to see inside.

Unconsciously, she looked towards the front door where the key sat in its lock, turned ninety degrees to prevent another one from working if it was inserted from the outside. She had stopped leaving the smaller kitchen window ajar. All the windows were kept locked now. She had positioned a large, deep-pile rug in the hallway so that it couldn't be avoided when entering the front door. She kept the pile carefully vacuumed in straight lines, like a well-maintained bowling green, so that any footfall would be immediately visible – an alert for any unauthorised entry.

Despite the improvised security measures, Lucy still found it hard to settle. When she did sleep, any small sound woke her and placed her on high alert, expecting to find Danny standing angrily over her. She was having more nightmares. Violent in nature: a recurring one where she searched an abandoned building, eventually finding members of her family who had been tortured, lying in pools of their own blood. She would wake with her heart pounding, body damp with sweat, peering into the darkest corners of her bedroom, then find it impossible to go back to sleep.

Starting to feel restless again, Lucy went through her extra night-time routine, placing glass tumblers behind windows, ornaments behind doors and a decorative china bell behind the front door. The home-made early warning system gave her small peace of mind. Since he had told her about waiting outside the flat, she rarely switched the lights on, trying to keep her presence hidden. She relied on sodium streetlights shining through the blinds, the floors were uncluttered so that she could move around easily. She knew it was unhealthy, but figured it was only short term and that she would be able to stop the precautions as soon as Danny got fed up and stopped contacting her.

Lucy took care to vary her route home, taking different roads and parking away from her flat. At least her surveillance training was useful for something, she thought glumly.

Getting back to the task of packing for the weekend, Lucy pulled a pair of walking trousers and some t-shirts from a chest of drawers, looking forward to putting some distance between her and the flat and to catching up with Fiona.

Early the next morning, Lucy stood in the street outside her flat. Dawn had not yet broken, but they needed to leave early for the ferry and the port was some distance away. Standing in the still morning air, she breathed in the smell of grass clippings and watched a fox slink under a hedge, rustling leaves as it went until Fiona brought her car to a gentle halt next to her. As Lucy settled into the front passenger seat, she indicated a takeaway coffee cup.

'There you go. That'll wake you up,' she said, pulling away from the kerb.

'Wow, good service,' Lucy told her with a smile.

'The boot's full of wood, so don't worry if you hear anything move around,' Fiona said, through sips of her own coffee.

Answering the confused look on Lucy's face, Fiona explained that her aunt Kathy had flatly refused to accept any payment for them to stay in her brand-new holiday pod, but Fiona knew that she wouldn't refuse a gift of logs for the wood-burning stoves in the house and the pod, so she had brought the wood and some groceries in exchange for their accommodation.

When Danny's name came up in conversation, Lucy told her that they had broken up. Fiona glanced at Lucy's face, gauging how much to say.

'Is it too early to say that I'm not sorry?' Fiona said.

Lucy picked at the plastic top of her coffee cup and asked why she thought so.

'I just never saw the attraction,' she said honestly. 'Too much baggage, too much hassle and an angry ex-wife.'

Lucy sighed again before she said, 'Not quite so *ex* as it turned out.'

Turning sharply to look at her, Fiona gripped the wheel and shook her head angrily. Finding it easier to speak sitting side by side in the car than on the phone, Lucy filled Fiona in on what she had kept secret. She gave an open and honest roundup of events, squirming uncomfortably when she got to the point where he'd punched her in the face and knocked her to the pavement. Fiona said nothing but let her talk, listening intently.

'You need to report it,' she said finally.

'There's no way I'm doing that,' Lucy said.

'What are you afraid of?' Fiona asked.

'I don't want to get him into trouble. He has a family to provide for. He can't afford to lose his job. It would be bound to backfire on me too. What if they didn't believe me, or said that I caused it? What if it went as far as court? The commander would want to distance the agency from me and any bad publicity. I'd be moved sideways or sent to some dead-end post, career over. How do you think Danny would react? I don't fancy my chances if he got really angry – and he would.' Lucy put down her empty coffee cup, shrugged and added, 'And that's if I was listened to. Don't forget he's very friendly with the commander. There's no doubt whose side he would come down on.'

Fiona understood, even if she didn't agree.

'Just think about it,' Fiona said.

Rolling off the ferry onto the island in the bright sunny morning, Lucy drank in the sparkling turquoise waters, pale sand, and lush green hills.

'Beautiful!'

'I know,' said Fiona, 'and this isn't even the prettiest part of the island.'

Fiona's aunt, Kathy, greeted them warmly at her house then chastised them for bringing wood and supplies. After they'd emptied the car of logs, Kathy handed them a mug of tea and set down a freshly made clementine cake. Lucy got up to admire deep blue paintings hanging on the white walls, as Kathy and Fiona caught up with family news.

Later, Fiona unpacked while Lucy opened the French windows of their well-appointed, wooden holiday home and walked out onto the deck, enjoying the fresh sea breeze whipping all around her. She admired the uninterrupted sea view and felt that she finally properly understood the phrase 'blowing away the cobwebs'. The effect was magical. Uplifting and invigorating. Lucy's hand instinctively checked her pocket for the presence of her mobile phone. Pulling it out, she realised that for the first time since they had split up, she had received no unwanted texts that morning. Maybe Danny had moved on she thought hopefully. Checking the screen, she saw that she had no signal and happily registered that she was free of her phone for the first time in ages, thinking that it was more of a noose than a lifeline these days. Brightening up, she switched it off and jammed it into her pocket before stepping down onto the dazzling white sand. Standing with the wind tossing her hair, watching white-capped waves roll onto the beach she exhaled and felt tension leave her. Feeling content and safe, she pulled off her boots and socks, left them on the deck and walked to the water's edge.

15.

Before the ferry home had docked, Lucy switched on her mobile phone. Jaw clenched, she watched as a string of notifications ran across the screen. She had been out of contact for little more than twenty-four hours, but twenty-seven messages now sat impatiently waiting for her attention. Every single one was from Danny. Aware of Fiona's gaze, Lucy switched it straight off again and pocketed it, not yet ready to return to everyday life.

Lucy asked Fiona to drop her off at the corner shop, a couple of streets away from the flat, instinctively wanting to keep her friend away in case he should be hanging around. She picked up a pint of milk and a loaf of bread, even though they would probably just sit about, like the last lot, until they were thrown away. Her appetite had vanished, and she was trying to stay away from home as much as possible, Danny's texts made her feel like a sitting duck at the flat.

When she did arrive home, Lucy fed the washing machine, pulled on some gym clothes, grabbed her bag and keys, and left again. She had already carried out a quick assessment of the flat and been satisfied that no one had been inside while she had been away, but it felt soulless and cold. She wanted to be surrounded by light, bustle and people, but without the need to converse. She made sure to wear headphones to deter even the smallest of polite conversation. Lucy turned up her music and increased the speed of the treadmill.

Driving home later, Lucy felt pleasantly tired, her muscles ached in a healthy way and her head was still full of beautiful images of the sea. She hoped it would help her sleep. Breaking her own rules, she parked in the designated bay outside the flat, feeling bolder, but she still hesitated before unlocking the car and climbing out. She looked for Danny, scanning the car park and garden shrubs, but the coast was clear. Releasing the breath she was holding, she walked quickly, covering the short distance to the front door with her gym bag in one hand, and a bunch of keys balled in the other, some protruding from between her fingers, as an improvised weapon to give her confidence.

Lucy opened drawers and rooted about, packing again. She was due to work at the Scottish Police College's Tulliallan Castle for the next couple of weeks, delivering covert surveillance training to detectives. She was a last-minute substitution to replace a colleague who had gone off sick. When she had worked there before, she had commuted to the castle, enjoying steady dayshift hours and her own bed, but with the flat a less appealing option, she decided to take up the offered room and stay on campus. Chris had been apologetic when he'd called to ask her to step in but he was happy to take any updates for Operation Flame and he'd keep her up to date. Not that there seemed to be much happening. Even Robbie Gillies's flat had quietened down with Lee still absent. They expected a decent haul of drugs to be brought in soon. There was the train courier's package to replace and demand would not have dwindled, but since Lee's disappearance, the inward flow had slowed down. Lucy was sure they'd get a break soon;

the Aitchisons couldn't risk that a rival outfit might step in and steal business away.

Early the next morning, Lucy stopped her car at the security barrier of the police college. She showed her ID to a cheerful member of security at the gate and took the proffered staff parking badge. A grey squirrel zig-zagged in front of her as she drove towards the castle, a large grey imposing structure in impressive vast, well-maintained gardens. Large grassy areas were bordered by brightly flowering rhododendron bushes and towering ancient trees.

Lucy parked and walked into the castle reception and along familiar oak panelled corridors, past suits of armour and trophy cabinets. As she moved further from the main entrance, the grandeur lessened until the decor became worn linoleum flooring with an empty plastic margarine tub collecting rainwater from an area of crumbling ceiling. The corridors were draughty and held on to a distinct smell of cleaning fluid and damp dog. No animals roamed the castle, the smell came from the fabric of the building and soggy probationary officers on basic training courses who ran endless loops of the castle grounds in constant Scottish drizzle.

Lucy's department was tucked away from the main castle and junior training. They joked that it was to prevent probationers or 'real police officers' from being tainted by CID.

Lucy had left her bags in the car, she'd have plenty of time to unpack in the evening after her class finished for the day. She collected keys for her room, clipped them to her ID lanyard and walked along the long, glass-walled, main corridor which overlooked the expanse of tarmacked parade square. As she neared the dining hall, the damp-dog scent mixed with an unappealing school dinners smell. Cursing her timing, the doors from the canteen flew open as dozens of smart, keen new officers poured out into the corridor. Every face turned to Lucy's, and she was engulfed in a sea of individual greetings of 'Ma'am'. Part of the old college tradition encouraged officers on basic training to acknowledge every person they encountered. Any officer wearing uniform of a higher rank would be referred to by their position but anyone not in uniform, as in Lucy's case, was greeted with 'Sir' or 'Ma'am'. Lucy had found it slightly amusing at first, but the novelty had soon worn off. Some of her colleagues revelled in being called 'Sir' or 'Ma'am', although they were the same rank as the constables who passed them. The only difference between them was that they had been in the job longer and wore plain clothes. Some bosses were extremely precious of their rank, insisting on being always addressed by it, but Lucy had never found this applied to the best of her supervisors.

Even in a castle, surrounded by police officers, Lucy couldn't stop being ultra security conscious. She was pleased to find her room was on the first floor. Having honed her college survival skills over many years, she opened a window of the stuffy room, then took a plug-in air freshener from her handbag and set it to work. She opened the cupboard doors wide, releasing a waft of stale odour from the previous occupant. Leaving the doors open to air all day, she propped open the door of a tiny ensuite room, which held a shower so small that she doubted she would have room to bend for a bar of soap if she dropped one. Satisfied, Lucy locked the room and made her way to the Starbucks counter where she purchased supplies for herself and Dale, an old colleague who would be joining her as a trainer.

The students seemed like a decent bunch overall. Many were new to CID and were unknown to Lucy. As she sat at the back of the classroom, listening to Dale open the course, run through the safety briefing and list of 'dos and don'ts', her phone vibrated with an incoming message. Checking the screen, she saw Chris Summers's name and opened the text to read that she wasn't missing anything back at base. No new intelligence or updates had come in for their drugs operation, but Chris assured her that he would keep in touch and that she should enjoy the *holiday* at *Castle Greyskull*. Lucy was relieved to see there were no new messages from Danny. She still wasn't replying to any of his texts, but it didn't seem to deter him – he could hold a completely one-sided conversation without any input from her. She pushed it all to the back of her mind, getting to her feet to address the class and start the first lesson.

Lucy enjoyed teaching, she was good at it, and being able to pass on practical experience, alongside classroom input, gave her a credibility that some of the full-time college staff lacked. She also liked the social element of being able to catch up with colleagues from other areas when they came together to take a course. There was time to chat and catch up over a drink at one of the local hostelries.

By mid-week, Danny's text messages had increased in number again, to such an extent that Lucy took to switching off her phone, only turning it on during breaks and in the evening for minimal distraction. Sitting at a desk in the training office, eating a thin cheese sandwich from the canteen, Lucy didn't pick up when her phone rang showing Danny's name on the caller ID. She left it to buzz and vibrate itself across the desk towards a mug of cold coffee instead. A voicemail message followed. Lucy's stomach tightened, but she grabbed the phone and played the short voicemail message. Danny's words were broken, he must have made the call while driving through an area with a patchy signal, but she was able to catch the gist of it, which was that he had been in touch with the garage to collect his newly repaired car, but needed her help, it was booked in under her name and he said they were refusing to give it to him and he needed it ASAP. Could she meet him on Saturday morning and go with him to collect it? Letting out an audible sigh, Lucy didn't know why the garage were being awkward. Nothing about his blasted car had been straight forward. She discarded the remains of her curling sandwich, swallowed a mouthful of cold coffee and dialled Danny's number. He answered it on the first ring, catching her off guard. He was pleasant as they made plans, but Lucy kept it brief, telling him that she was at work and in a hurry. He took it well, not even protesting when she asked him not to contact her again unless he had to cancel their Saturday morning plans. Ending the call, Lucy looked at the phone and tapped a finger on the desk, imagining a future where she could leave her phone on all the time and lose the feeling of dread which came with every notification. Maybe he had finally come to terms with the end of their relationship?

16.

When Lucy collected Danny on Saturday morning, from outside a coffee shop in town, it was with a feeling of trepidation, despite the neutral territory. As he got in the car, he was accompanied by a cloud of expensive-smelling aftershave. He was well-groomed, all smiles and had the familiarity of an old friend. He told her how good it was to see her and complimented her on how well she looked. When she held a hand up, palm open towards him, he apologised, and said, 'Okay. Too much. I'll shut up.'

He seemed excited, in a good mood and chattered all the way to the garage, telling her that things hadn't worked out with Susan in the end. He had been sleeping at his friend Paul's house, travelling back and forth to take care of his children.

As they reached the garage, Danny sheepishly told Lucy that money was still tight for him and asked if she would pay the invoice, promising to reimburse her as soon as he could. Lucy had already suspected as much, guessing that it was the real reason that Danny had asked her to take him to the garage, doubting they would care who the car was handed to, as long as the bill was paid.

Lucy stood at the service desk with a grimy mechanic

who wiped a hand on the leg of a dirty boiler suit, before counting out the cash he'd asked for in exchange for a slight discount. It had been worth the bother of nipping out to the bank. She didn't ask for a receipt and none was offered. As she turned to leave, she casually asked, 'Did you need me here, or would you have given the car to him?' nodding towards where Danny sat, perched on the only customer chair, scrolling through his phone.

'No, lass,' he chuckled, pushing a grubby black woollen beanie hat towards the back of his head, 'Like I told him on the phone, I just want it gone. I need the space and I've got wages to pay.'

Thanking him and noting Danny's lie, Lucy wondered if he wanted her cash, her company or both?

Standing next to his car, the engine idling, Danny's enthusiasm was contagious and despite her misgivings, Lucy felt herself drawn towards him and grinning back.

'Come on, let's go for a wee spin. Make sure it's definitely fixed?' Danny asked her.

Seeing the smile slide off her face and her body stiffen, he cajoled, 'Please? Pretty please? Let me at least buy you a coffee, then?'

She was surprised to hear herself agree. Locking her own car and leaving it on the street outside the garage, Lucy grabbed her handbag and climbed into the passenger seat of Danny's car.

'They could have washed it at least,' she muttered, taking in the dusty paintwork.

Driving past the row of shops with their favourite coffee shop, Danny told her that they were going to the carwash first.

A short time later, they sat quietly together in his car, jolting through the noisy, mechanical contraption, brushes whirring and pummelling as water whooshed and hissed all around them.

Lucy said, 'I hope this clown car doesn't fall apart.'

Danny looked at her in mock affront, then said, 'I know! It's probably only the rust that's holding it together.'

Laughing, they made proper eye contact for the first time that day and Lucy found herself warming to him.

'I miss you,' Danny told her, taking her hand in both of his, while they trundled along. Planting a tender kiss on the back of her hand, he seized the moment, 'I know! Let's go on a road trip. Let's properly test the car and we can catch up.'

Lucy looked doubtfully at his happy face but was struck with a melancholic nostalgia that this was the same person, who only a few weeks ago, she had thought she would spend the rest of her life with. Without considering it further, she nodded slowly in agreement.

The journey passed in a steady stream of reminiscing and banter and before she knew it, they had crossed the border into England, where the sun was waiting to greet them. The first small market town they entered was utterly charming with old sandstone buildings and floral planters. Bunting hung cheerfully over the main street, giving the place a happy, holiday mood.

'I'm starving,' said Danny, parking in the village square near a characterful Inn, pointing at it and saying, 'Let's have an early dinner there.'

As Lucy tucked into a tasty steak-and-ale pie, the waiter delivered a bottle of champagne in an ice bucket to their table. Lucy looked at Danny, her forehead wrinkled. They were driving, so the alcohol couldn't be for them, surely? Danny's wide smile told her that it was. As her mouth opened and closed, goldfish-like, he grabbed her hand, telling her, 'I ordered it. Let's celebrate. It's been such a good day and I feel like we're at the start of something special.'

Lucy closed her mouth, and managed to reply, 'But we're driving.'

Danny awkwardly pulled a key from his pocket. It was attached to an oversize, plastic keyring bearing the name of the Inn.

'I've got us a room. We're staying,' he beamed. Something uneasy shifted inside Lucy but she felt an undeniable pull of attraction, recognising the spontaneous, impulsive side of Danny's nature that she loved. It made her want to embrace life, to live it fully, and feel that she had grabbed every opportunity it offered. Weighing it up while studying his face, Lucy chewed her bottom lip. Danny took her hesitancy as suspicion, reassuring her that he and Susan were finished. There was no hope for their relationship. In fact, they couldn't even bear to be under the same roof. He looked deep into her eyes, searching, telling her that she was all he had ever wanted and that he was sorry for having made such a stupid mistake. Losing her had caused the worst pain in his life and he couldn't live without her. Pouring champagne and handing a glass to Lucy, he intoned, 'I promise, I'll never let you down.'

Six hours and several drinks later Danny was well oiled. Not completely pie-eyed, but sloppily drunk. He had been standing at the bar, talking to strangers, leaning towards them, slurring words of bonhomie in an overfamiliar way, oblivious to their discomfort and the smiles behind his back. It seemed to Lucy that with every drink Danny had his mood amplified. She hated it and had stopped drinking earlier, not that he had noticed. He had been too busy holding court, downing pints and handing out unsolicited points of view on everything from private education to football teams. It was a habit of his to place his mobile telephone on whatever table or bar he sat at. Danny had ignored his phone all evening, but Lucy had seen a stream of text-message notifications pass across the screen, and now Susan's name lit up as she called his number. Scowling at the phone, at first to focus and read the screen, and then in disgust, Danny jabbed at it, rejecting the call. Lucy looked at him, trying and failing to see the man she had once fallen for. Eventually Danny got to his feet, slightly unsteadily, picked up his phone and headed for the door. Guessing that he was about to call Susan, and wanting no part in their drama, Lucy remained where she was, working out what she would do, harbouring a sinking feeling that she had made a mistake. She let out a puff of air, shaking her head to herself, realising that what she was seeing was the real Danny. He was not an exciting, impulsive and spontaneous character. Just immature and chaotic.

As a member of staff cleared the empty glasses from a nearby table, trailing a dirty, wet rag half-heartedly over the surface, Lucy asked her about bus travel back to Scotland. She deeply regretted having had a drink. She had too much alcohol in her system to drive home right now, even if Danny did agree to it. She criticized herself for having relented and gone with him. Learning that there would be no bus until ten o'clock the next morning, she cursed. She was stuck here, unable to get herself home. Lucy calculated that Danny was unlikely to be sober enough to drive early the next morning, but she would be. She would get on the road as soon as she could rouse him, leaving before the first bus.

Danny returned to the bar, reached for a pint glass and offered no explanation for his ten-minute absence. Lucy read his face for clues, but only found an arrogant and slightly vacant look in his eyes. Draining his glass, Danny asked if she wanted another drink, but his words were drowned out by a clanging bell announcing last orders.

Lucy declined, pointing to her nearly full glass of flat lemonade as Danny signalled for one more pint.

Later, at the door of their room, Danny paused, 'It's only small. It was the last one they had. They don't usually let it out; we were lucky to get it.'

The door swung open to reveal a tiny attic bedroom, so small that it made her room at Tulliallan Castle feel like a suite. A single bed stood against the wall to the left side and a tub chair sat behind the open door, preventing it from fully opening. There was a small window, framed by curtains stiff with dust, directly across from the door. She saw that a door on the wall opposite the bed, gave access to an ensuite bathroom, which was almost the same size as the bedroom. Although narrow, it had a full-sized bath and a large, old-fashioned white sink and toilet.

'I know, I know,' Danny said, walking inside and filling the room. 'But it'll be cosy.'

Lucy wrestled with the window frame which had swollen closed, managing to prize it slightly open and let some cool night air into the stifling room. An old metal radiator under the window was hot to the touch as she leaned against it for leverage to open the window. Trying and failing to turn it off, Lucy walked into the bathroom. Without a toothbrush, she ran the sink tap, gulping mouthfuls of water, gargling and rinsing her mouth as best she could. The old enamelled bath had a yellowing, white-gloss plywood panel nailed to its side. Dust had settled on the bathroom surfaces. A worn, but clean towel hung over the piping-hot bathroom radiator. Lucy wiped her mouth on it and then walked two paces back into the bedroom where Danny sat on the edge of the bed, removing his trainers. Running his hands through his hair, he told Lucy that he missed the big bathroom in their flat and was looking forward to a powerful shower when they got home.

Lucy's eyes widened and she swallowed nervously. There was no way he was moving back into the flat, but now was not the time to have that discussion, especially in the doll's-house room with its paper-thin walls. As if reading her mind, and in defiance, Danny deliberately raised his voice, a completely unnecessary act when there was so little distance between them. Getting to his feet and towering over her even with his shoes off, his voice dripped sarcasm, and his eyes narrowed as he said, 'Oh, no. You've got to be joking. You were just stringing me along?'

Not waiting for an answer, he shouldered her easily out of his path, causing her to stumble as he entered the bathroom, leaving the door open, urinating loudly while carrying on a one-sided conversation, getting louder and angrier with every word he spat out.

Lucy's blood ran cold. Her heart rate quickened and a low hum began in her ears as she started to worry, realising she was trapped. She sat down on the bed before her jelly legs could give way. She didn't dare leave the room. She didn't want to trigger him further. He was already so angry that she feared he would shout and cause such a scene that they would be thrown out, or the police would be called. There was no seating area at the reception desk and the public areas were closed. There was nowhere else for her to go. Danny strode back into the bedroom, feet thumping on the thin carpeted floor, and began to pace back and forth, like a caged animal. Reading his body language, Lucy's breathing became shallow and rapid as she struggled to remain composed. She avoided eye contact, staring at a patch of carpet in front of her. Danny's mouth was small, his lips tight and curled. His arms hung tense at his sides and his fists clenched and unclenched as he paced, uttering sharp, angry words.

'Bitch!' he snarled through gritted teeth, spittle landing on Lucy's face as he grabbed her by the shoulders, roughly pulling her to her feet.

Lucy thought she might be able to speak to him, to somehow calm the rage, but her mouth was dry and panic had lodged the words in her tight throat, leaving her mute. Wishing feverishly that she had left the room when she had the chance, she eyed the door to the hallway, just a few feet away. Danny spun her round so that she was facing him. She saw that his face was flushed, his eyes were blazing and gummy spit had collected in the corners of his mouth. Fear rooted her to the spot. He didn't need to keep hold of her, but he did. She could feel his fingers digging into her upper arms. What had happened to her fight or flight reflex? she wondered dully, cursing herself inwardly for being temporarily incapable of either. Letting go of her he took a step backwards towards the bathroom. Before she had time to think anything else, he flew at her and screamed, 'You fucking bitch!' as he closed the short distance between them, shoving her on the chest with two hands. Falling backwards, Lucy expected to hit the floor but was momentarily relieved to feel the side of the narrow, spongy bed at the back of her legs, but she sailed on, until the back of her head cracked against the bedroom wall. She slumped, landing half on and half off the end of the bed. Before she could rearrange herself, Danny hauled her to her feet again. She had a floating feeling, almost as if she was dancing, with her feet hardly touching the ground before she was thrown with some force against the wall at the foot of the bed. Lucy let out an involuntary gasp as her body collided heavily with the wall and air left her lungs. Falling to the dusty, carpeted floor, Lucy tried to gather herself into a ball. With her back against the high wooden skirting board and knees at her chest, she watched Danny walk backwards for as many steps as he could, until the heel of his left, sock-clad foot, hit the plyboard bath panel. Then he ran at her, over the mercifully short distance, kicking her with as much force as he could muster. Lucy shut her eyes tight, hearing the crack of bone, unsure whether it was his foot or her ribs. She felt entirely numb. She felt stupidly grateful that he'd removed his shoes. As if she was watching the scene from somewhere above, she saw herself being kicked again and punched on the head until suddenly there was a loud knocking at the door.

Time seemed to stand still. Lucy was terrified, biting her lower lip to stop herself whimpering. Danny tried to ignore the now persistent banging, but then heard a jangle of keys at the door and accompanied shout, 'This is the manager. I'm coming in!'

Danny's shoulders dropped, his posture relaxed and he raked his fingers through his hair, shouting back, 'We're fine here, pal.'

Lucy swallowed hard, praying that the man on the other side of the door would come in and at least cause a diversion whereby she could escape. She felt as if she was glued to the carpet. Her troubled mind told her to lie still, to stay quiet, that she didn't want the police to be called.

Immobile with fear, feeling heavy-limbed and cold, Lucy became aware of Danny hissing in her ear, 'Get up!'

The words released another layer of terror in her, immediately transporting her back to the cold, grey pavement where she had lain after he'd hit her the first time. Trembling uncontrollably, she tried and failed to make herself move. She wondered if she had been hurt badly enough to have sustained a spinal injury when her back had struck the skirting board, but as Danny lifted her up, propping her on the bed, with her back against the wall, she felt every fibre in her body. The sound of a key turning in the lock made Danny rush to open it a crack, standing behind the door, barring entry. The door opened just enough for Lucy to see a dishevelled man, the one who had identified himself as the manager. He didn't look much older than her and had the appearance of someone who had been woken from sleep. Another, slightly younger man stood behind him, wide-eyed and silent. Lucy recognised him as being one of the waiters she had seen earlier. The manager looked pointedly past Danny, into the room, his eyes finding Lucy. He asked if she was alright. Lucy found herself unable to speak. Her teeth chattered and she desperately tried to hold herself together. She managed to give a small nod, hoping that would suffice.

'Well, I'd better not hear another peep from you two tonight, or you're out.' He addressed Danny, who assured him that he wouldn't and the door closed. Lucy was exhausted, limp and sore. Completely spent, she slid down the wall, curling up on the end of the bed, sobbing quietly.

Danny sat at the other end of the bed, examining his fist, checking himself for any injury. Leaning back against the headboard, he stretched his legs out in front of him, causing Lucy to flinch at the sight of his white sports socks close to her. Getting strength from the need to distance herself from him, Lucy pushed herself up, got shakily to her feet and went into the bathroom, locking the thin door behind her. She knew that the sliding bolt wouldn't be enough to keep Danny out, but it was all she had. She vomited into the toilet bowl, feeling a sharp, stabbing pain in her ribs as she did so.

The rage seemed to have left Danny. He hadn't been drunk enough to challenge the hotel staff to fight, and was sober enough to realise that he didn't want them to involve the police, so he would keep his hands off Lucy now.

Getting up and rinsing vomit from her mouth, Lucy was

still shaking. She grabbed the towel from the radiator, pulled it around her shoulders and sat on the bathroom floor, watching the door. Her heart raced, and her mind was a useless jumble of broken thoughts. She held her breath, trembling and listening until she heard snoring from the bedroom. She was out of danger for now.

The next morning, Lucy got up stiffly from the bathroom floor. Every part of her body hurt. She splashed cold water on her face and rinsed out her mouth. Then she carried out a head-to-toe self-assessment. Her head throbbed, her scalp was tender with lumps and bumps, her neck ached. Her ribs were sore and her back hurt where it had connected with the skirting board and the wall. Her left forearm had already started to bruise and the elbow joint was swollen and painful to move. Fingerprint bruising was beginning to emerge on both her upper arms where she had been held. Her left shin, buttock and hip still smarted from kicks. She limped over to peer into the small mirror, checking for marks to her face, relieved to find none.

Remembering the looks on the faces of the hotel staff, Lucy's face flushed with shame and fresh tears welled in her red-rimmed eyes. Forcing herself to get a grip, she blinked away tears, took a deep breath and released it slowly as she unbolted and opened the bathroom door. Danny lay on his back on the single bed, under the duvet, sound asleep. His clothes were strewn on the floor. Lucy heard a nearby pipe creak into life and a toilet flush in the room next door. The noise was distinct, and so easy to hear that Lucy knew the occupants must been aware of the disturbance. Even if they had been asleep, it would easily have woken them. Perhaps they had made the call to the staff.

Lucy gently pushed Danny's exposed right shoulder and whispered, 'Wake up. We need to go.'

Shrugging the duvet over his shoulder, Danny murmured something unintelligible. They had to leave as soon as possible, before everyone else got up and went about their Sunday morning. Lucy told him as much, and he sat up slowly, rubbing his eyes and lumbered off to the bathroom, while she gathered his clothes to speed their departure. When Danny returned from the bathroom, he said nothing to Lucy, and she had no desire to converse with him. She simply picked up his car keys and said, 'I'll drive. Come on.'

As he dressed, Lucy pulled back the duvet to air the bed, revealing a wet patch on the bottom sheet. Numbly and swiftly, she ignored the pain in her arm and ribs, pulled it off the bed, balled it up and left it in the bath with the damp towel.

Feeling as if she was on autopilot, falling back into damage-limitation mode, Lucy opened the door, checked to ensure that no one was about and crept down two flights of stairs, past the vacant reception desk, towards the exit. Slipping out of the building, with Danny in tow, she squinted in the early morning sun and walked to Danny's car. Wordlessly, they both got in and she drove them away.

17.

As soon as Lucy had parked up behind her own car, she could not wait to get away from the crumpled shell of Danny, who sat next to her. Numbness and shock were beginning to wear off, swiftly replaced by revulsion. She killed the engine, turning to take a final look at him. He couldn't meet her eye. She got out of his car and limped to the driver's door of hers. She wanted to hold her head up high, to stride away, but in the end, she was sore and defeated, struggling to move and miserable tears stung her eyes. She no longer cared how she looked or what he thought of her. Before she had managed to fasten her seatbelt, she heard Danny's engine start and the crunch of grit under tyres as he drove away.

As Lucy rolled into the parking bay at her flat, she looked up at the building's many windows, checking for any signs of life. It was still early and there was no evidence of her neighbours, the whole place was quiet and subdued. She had never met any of them and suspected that, like her, their apartments were a convenient base, not a real home. The newly built estate comprised a handful of large, detached houses and several blocks of matching flats in landscaped grounds. The estate agent referred to these as 'lifestyle villas and apartment buildings in an exclusive area' their own longhand for 'expensive to rent'. The location was desirable, with easy transport links to all the major cities and a selection of high-end shops, restaurants, and bars a short taxi ride away. There were always some vacant flats with agency signs hanging from windows, and even the ones which were occupied had a constant carousel of transient tenants move through them. The overall effect was impressive but characterless. Nobody knew or conversed with their neighbours, Lucy had seen so little of the others in her own block that she wouldn't have been able to pick out any of them from a line-up and she expected she was a stranger to them too.

Lucy closed her front door, automatically turning the key its customary ninety degrees in the lock. She scrubbed her teeth clean and while a hot bath ran, she went about the flat taking stock of what possessions she still had there. She resolved to empty the flat, moving boxes of her possessions to her parents' house piece by piece, until the flat was empty of all but the original furnishings. Then she would call the letting agency and return it. She no longer cared about the last few months of rent, which would still have to be paid. It could sit empty, she just wanted rid of it.

Lucy eased her sore body into a eucalyptus-scented bath, which was as hot as she could stand, and began scrubbing her skin. She'd clean up then return to Tulliallan Castle for the night, study the waiting phone updates for operation Flame and get ready to deliver the last week of surveillance training. She might as well be productive while she kept herself distracted from the car crash of her personal life. She was already concocting suitable excuses for her aches, pains and restricted movement. She would be sure to wear clothes which covered the already colourful assortment of bruises on her body and pick up a pack of ibuprofen tablets to go with the paracetamol she already had. If anyone mentioned her undeniable limp, she would tell them that she had a bad back and that it had flared up.

Before leaving, Lucy ensured that all the window and door traps were set. She had less idea than before what Danny was capable of, and couldn't be sure that he'd stay away. She swallowed hard, remembering again his face, his fists and his feet from the previous night's assault. It made her queasy. The thought of her colleagues and of her family and friends finding out what had happened made her squirm with anxiety. She heaped blame on herself for the idiocy of going back to him, for placing herself in such a vulnerable position. She was absolutely certain that she would not let him back into her life again.

Settling back into her room at Tulliallan, Lucy felt safer and became overwhelmed by tiredness. Closing the curtains, she went to bed, not bothering with dinner. Grabbing her phone to set an alarm, she cringed to see that Danny had already sent several texts. Leaving them unread, she switched it off and closed her eyes, falling asleep almost immediately.

At 01:47 in the morning, Lucy woke up with a start. She wrestled off the covers and sat up, gasping for air. She was sweating, her heart thudded in her chest and her breathing came fast and shallow. She peered around the unfamiliar room, surfacing from a vivid nightmare. Remembering that she was in her room at the college, she got up and switched all the lights on, not satisfied that she was alone until she had thoroughly searched the small room and wardrobe. With her heart still pounding, she checked that the window was closed and the door locked. Her hip and elbow protested as she dragged and pushed a chair against the door. Unable to shake off the last of the nightmare, in which Danny had been pushing her from a

115

window, she picked up her mobile, switched it on and played some quiet music to fill the dark corners of her mind. Too wired to sleep, she made herself a cup of tea and sat at the desk, steeling herself before reluctantly opening the latest string of unread text messages.

There were seventeen in total, all from Danny. One was almost, but not quite, an apology in which he euphemistically referred to their trip away as a 'bad time'. Most contained the same, well-worn lines, about how much he missed her and how they should be together. A couple of them enquired where she was, suggesting that he had called round and found the flat empty. She ignored them all, leaving them unanswered, but they bothered her and buzzed around her brain like a bluebottle at a window.

Sipping her tea, she sat back, eyebrows knitted in contemplation. She put down the cup and grabbed an A4 book and a pen from her bag, feeling a compulsion to log all Danny's unwanted texts and calls. She unlocked her phone and began to transcribe all those which she had not yet deleted. She hoped that writing them down might clear them from her brain, at least enough to let her sleep again.

Two hours later, she had a chronological record of all the unwanted contact from Danny and had cleared her phone. She neatly listed the dates, times and whether it was a call, voicemail or text, writing out the content word for word. She transcribed the few messages that she had sent him or made a call. She checked these for context. Looking for any indication that she might have encouraged his behaviour or the unsolicited contact. She only saw short messages of the same, unambiguous wording, asking him to please stop contacting her. Leafing back over the pages of her book, Lucy regarded them all properly with her 'police head' on, as she did when sifting through data dumps for Operation Flame. She viewed the entries with fresh eyes, appalled at the volume and content. It was clear his habit was to bombard her with dozens of messages over the course of a day. These generally started as fawning, reminiscing about their time together, then became whingeing and full of self-pity, before turning curt, abusive and ultimately, threatening.

She was certain that had the hotel staff not intervened the night before, Danny would have carried on assaulting her until he was too tired to continue or he had killed her. The realisation was chilling. No wonder he was in her nightmares. Looking at the messages, she could see that he was angry. It was also apparent from the way that they continued, becoming darker and more menacing, that he believed she wouldn't report his criminal behaviour. He had even said as much in a few of the messages.

She carried out an honest appraisal of the threat he posed, as if she was a police officer called to investigate someone else's domestic abuse. Her mouth went dry as she graded her own 'case' threat level as high. She was stuck with the dilemma; believing that he could kill her but feeling unable to report him. She was still processing what had happened, not ready to tell anyone yet, not even Fiona, but what if he did kill her? He had plenty of charm and charisma. Her colleagues thought he was a great bloke and the commander loved him. Unless he was caught red-handed, nobody would suspect him. She still hoped that he might just leave her alone, but she feared the worst. Recent events had shown her that she had no idea what he was actually capable of.

Lucy decided to lock the notebook away in her desk drawer at work, buried under other books and documentation. It would remain safely hidden and private there, but if she died, her desk would be cleared out and it would be uncovered.

Settling back into bed with the desk light still on, serving as a night light, she satisfied herself that at least if he did murder her, she would have done the detective work for the police and they would know that it was premeditated, not a crime of passion nor a spur-of-the-moment, temporary loss of sanity. He wouldn't be able to deny it. With this as cold comfort, Lucy closed her eyes, determined to at least get some rest even if sleep eluded her. She dreaded having another nightmare but was unable to stay awake any longer.

18.

Lucy dropped to her knees, in a field, watching the dog twitch and convulse, his brown eyes wide open, staring and unseeing.

'No!' she exclaimed, over and over again, as she picked the creature up, gathering his warm, furry body in her arms, holding him against her sobbing chest.

Through her abject misery she sensed that someone crouched in the treeline, enjoying her devastation. She couldn't see him, but she knew it was Danny.

Gasping great sobs, Lucy woke, sitting up in bed, her empty arms still cradling a dead dog. She was shocked and panicked, her hair was damp with sweat. Her nightshirt clung to her skin and she was confused until she registered that it had been a nightmare. There was no dog, no field, no Danny. The dog in her dream, her family pet, had died years earlier of old age, after a long and happy life.

The time was 1.47 a.m. – the exact time she had woken, terrified and distressed, for the past three nights. She'd had different nightmares each time, but every single one had felt so real that she couldn't believe they hadn't actually occurred. The rawness of them clung to her and she could still feel them all through her waking hours, like a wound. It was exhausting. Her eyes were permanently dark ringed, feeling dry and gritty. Her skin was parched, and her body ached for sleep but when bedtime came, she didn't want to close her eyes for the fear of what was waiting in her dreams.

19.

Lucy was usually the first to arrive at the office, and today was no different. Stifling a yawn, punching numbers into the alarm control pad, she disarmed it. Switching on lights, she walked into the small kitchen area where she filled the kettle with fresh water and heaped two teaspoons of instant coffee into her mug. As the kettle boiled, she drained the basin, emptying cold, dirty water, using her fingers to corral an assortment of cutlery, cups and plates. Refilling the basin with hot water and a good squeeze of washing-up liquid, she washed and stacked everything, reaching for the grubby, stained tea towel, before she thought the better of it and left everything to air-dry. The cheap white, plastic kettle clicked off, steam billowing from its spout.

Lucy set a milk carton on the countertop while she opened the fridge. The garlic waft of salami from a long-forgotten opened packet hit her hard. She grabbed the offensive pack, wrapped it in a carrier bag and threw it in the bin. She checked the dates on three different pints of milk, discarded two immediately and sniffed the third gingerly. It was still in date, but she took nothing for granted. Placing the new milk in the fridge, she carried a mug of black coffee to her desk. She had managed to put herself right off milk today.

Lucy shrugged off her jacket, hung it over the back of her chair and put her handbag on the floor, toeing it out of the way while she unlocked the cabinet of drawers under her desk. As routinely as she had disarmed the office alarm and had made coffee, she opened the top drawer and pulled out the lined notebook in which she had been recording all of Danny's texts and calls for the last couple of weeks. Sighing deeply and unconsciously, she grabbed a pen, opened the book, jabbed at her mobile and added to the toll. When she had finished, Lucy replaced the book carefully under operational work. She logged onto the computer, sipped coffee and nodded a greeting to the first of her colleagues as they arrived.

'Kettle's just boiled,' Lucy said, as Roddy wandered into the office.

'Great,' he said, 'My head's full of banging doors. Bloody kids were a right pest last night. That's the second night this week I've had to babysit while the Mrs went off galivanting.'

'Roddy, I don't think you can call it *babysitting* when you're looking after your own children,' Lucy said, without looking up from her screen.

'Honestly, they're so annoying. Always whining, needing attention.'

'Well, it sounds like they're definitely yours anyway,' Inchy said, walking in.

Half an hour later, Lucy was summoned to Inchy's office where she found him behind his desk, flipping back through pages of his daybook. Opposite him, occupying one of the two visitor seats was Kelly, another detective from a different group. Lucy liked her; she was smart, funny, no-nonsense and good at her job.

'Right, girls,' Inchy said, still flicking through his daybook, missing Kelly's eye roll.

Lucy gave her a half-smile of agreement in reply.

'Your mission, should you choose to accept it ... well, no, you're getting it anyway. It seems our Lee Aitchison has made a guest appearance in Manchester.' He slid a black and white image over his desk for the detectives to study.

'Looks like him', Lucy said, moving closer to better study the grainy photograph.

'A mobile, belonging to him,' Inchy said, pointing to the image on the desk, 'has flagged with the National. They believe that he is trying to purchase a decent quantity of drugs from their current target.'

Kelly sat straighter in the chair, her interest piqued. The National Crime Unit was the surveillance outfit, which was to the UK what the Scottish Crime Agency was to Scotland. Most of their collective were English officers with only a few others from elsewhere making up their number.

'It would be mutually beneficial for you pair to join them for a short, technical job. One of the team has been nobbled and gone to the dark side,' Inchy told them, his finger finding scrawled notes in his book. 'There was a very convenient break-in to one of their motors. Covert radio sets with spare batteries and a complete operational file were taken when the unit's dodgy detective went for a toilet break.'

Kelly looked at Inchy, eager to get to the point. 'So they need a couple of new faces?'

'Yes. Lucy, you're going to sort out the tech on their subject's motor. Kelly, you're going to link their main man to a new bank account.'

He turned his book so that Lucy could read it, tapping his finger on the information she needed. Lucy noted the make, model and registration number of the subject's car.

'One off, one on,' he said.

In other words, she had to remove a covert tracking device and replace it with another. Lucy was already working out how quickly she could get her hands on a replica and a ramp to research the car before they had to leave.

'When are they expecting us?' she asked.

'Go tomorrow. Take a car from here and your own comms. They'll give you anything else you need when they brief you. Pack for a week. I've told them that's all I can spare you for. Kelly, if you can identify the subject's current banking details, the squad reckon that'll give them enough to freeze his assets under the Proceeds of Crime Act.'

Lucy looked up at him, nodding. 'Clever. A cash flow problem would disrupt the drugs supply up here to the Aitchisons, and the timing will appear suspicious when the police come knocking right after Lee, their newest customer, has paid a visit. Do they know where he is?'

'No, they haven't housed him.'

Lucy leaned back, smiling slowly. 'They've never sourced from Manchester before. They must be getting desperate.'

Over more coffee, Kelly and Lucy thrashed out logistics, then Lucy picked up her desk phone.

'I need a favour,' she said.

Later that day, Kelly dropped Lucy at the Audi garage. She enjoyed the short drive from there to the police workshop in Aberdeen, in the same model of car the subject owned. As she nosed the brand-new sports car inside, the technicians turned to stare, and the workshop manager greeted her with a long whistle, theatrically bowing and pointing to an empty hydraulic ramp.

'That was for the car, not you,' he said, as Lucy climbed out and walked over to join him at the control panel. He raised the car. 'Say when.'

'When!' Lucy told him.

She helped herself to a pair of orange disposable gloves

and got to work exploring the underside of the car. She wanted to familiarise herself with as much of it as possible, to identify the best hiding place for her tracker and practice putting it on. She could already see a couple of possibilities.

'Give me a shout if you need anything, and ask George over there, when you're ready to lower the ramp,' he told her.

Lucy took her time, exploring the underside of the car, keeping away from any hot or moving parts. Her fingers explored crevasses and ledges, looking for an ideal hiding place. She enjoyed being in the workshop, liked the order of it, tidy spaces with neatly stocked tool chests, background radio tunes punctuated by the hum and whirr of power tools. The team of technicians working in silence with an occasional shout or good-humoured ribbing. The smell of fuel and oil had a better relaxing effect on her than any spa fragrance.

The next day, Kelly and Lucy stood in a sparse office at the National Crime Unit. It looked like they had just moved in and had yet to unpack all the office equipment, or that they were ready to leave at short notice. They were briefed by a friendly detective inspector with a soft Geordie lilt, who explained to them that the operation had been paused since their kit and operational file had been stolen. Team morale was through the floor: one bad apple had caused them all to look at each other differently, seeking any sign of corruption, wondering if they could be bought or frightened into giving information to a criminal gang. A decision had been made to disband the team and they would never work with each other again. This was another bitter blow to the colleagues who were still reeling from their team-mate's deceit. He told them that the best result would be for their subject to be brought to justice and if it helped Operation Flame at the same time, so much the better.

Their subject was a well-established drug-dealer who had branched out into the motor trade. Cars and motorcycles were stolen to order by gangs of youths, who would then hand them over for amounts of cash that they would never be able to earn legitimately. The vehicles were broken-down and moved out of the country by the lorry load. If stopped and checked, the contents appeared to be a jumble of spare parts, reclaimed from damaged vehicles. If the whole lot was unloaded and reassembled, there were entire performance cars and motorcycles ready to sell on the black market abroad.

The business model had already made the subject and his associates extremely wealthy. They didn't bother to hide their riches, investing in luxury watch collections, wardrobes full of designer clothes and garages full of exotic cars, which would be the envy of any rapper. The main subject remained in the house he had grown up in. He had no desire to try and fit in elsewhere, finding it easier to keep a stranglehold on drug-dealing and street crime, in the area where he knew, and was known to, everyone. It provided him with an extra ring of security. Any new face stuck out like a sore thumb, and was quickly spotted by children on bicycles, who he paid to keep a sharp eye out. The last thing he and his community wanted was police, social workers or any such undesirables in the area. Even the youngest employees looked menacing, leaning against lamp posts, hoods up, fanning themselves with banknotes and overtly handling at least two mobile phones, one for the 'job' and another of their own.

Lucy and Kelly understood the risks of this deployment. They always worked under the assumption that their subject was either surveillance-aware or paranoid, but this job was harder since the subject was now fully aware of the ongoing operation. Instead of curbing his illegal activity, the subject

126

had become increasingly blasé, feeling that he had the upper hand and he was invincible.

They planned to have him traced and followed by a mobile surveillance team, which would be no mean feat. Lucy and Kelly would follow on, waiting until a suitable opportunity presented itself to move in and carry out the trickier vehicle and financial tasks. Settling in for a long wait, Lucy pulled the well-travelled novel from her bag, checked the silent radio was working, and began to read.

Only twenty minutes later, a crackle of static over the radio made them jump into action. Kelly tipped out the remaining half of her takeaway coffee, Lucy stowed her book, pulling out a map and a laptop in anticipation of movement. They listened intently to the radio traffic, hearing the surveillance team's updates, following the route as the subject casually left his home and drove to visit one of his girlfriends. He remained parked on the street outside her house with the Audi's engine idling, while he checked his phone. Impatiently, he blasted the horn causing a young, blonde woman to emerge from the address, struggling to walk quickly in a pair of high heels and short skirt. She climbed into his car and was driven off at speed before she could even fasten her seatbelt. The convoy headed for the motorway, with Kelly and Lucy following at a distance. Lucy readied her tracker device, carefully placing it in her handbag as Kelly sped them along the road. They sat in silence, concentrating.

Lucy's heart rate increased to a steady thump with anticipation. She licked dry lips, examining the area ahead on the map, seeking a possible destination. They assumed the trip would be for pleasure rather than for business when the subject had collected his female passenger. She hadn't even brought a coat with her, making Lucy think it would be a fairly local destination they'd visit. The surveillance team gave early warning as the subject approached a motorway exit, signalling left for the junction. None of the team would commit to leaving the motorway until the Audi definitely took the exit. It was one of the basics Lucy taught her surveillance students. At least once on every course she had instructed, an overeager student had ended up with egg on their face by committing themselves to taking a junction, only to watch the subject vehicle return to the main carriageway at the last moment. When Lucy played the part of the subject during training, she made sure to give the squad car a cheery wave as the occupants looked at her aghast, as they sailed off, down the wrong road. A hard, but good lesson, ensuring they were never 'sold a dummy' in real life. Sometimes students were so determined not to lose the subject that they doggedly followed on, swerving out of the exit lane – attracting the attention of the subject and everyone else on the road.

The Audi took the exit with no funny business, leaving the motorway, while Lucy searched the map with her fingertips.

'Retail Park ahead,' she let Kelly know.

'Could be,' Kelly replied.

As the Audi pulled into the sizable, almost empty car park of an out-of-town retail park, they held back listening to radio updates.

'Blue parking lot, near a big TK Maxx,' Lucy relayed to Kelly as she manoeuvred them closer to the action.

Kelly found them a suitable parking spot and they held their breath, waiting and checking other vehicles entering, looking for any sign of association with their subject.

'Coast clear. I'm away,' Lucy told Kelly, inserting her earpiece. She closed the car door noiselessly and crossed the car park. Hearing that the subject and his girlfriend had entered the shop, trailed by a surveillance operative, with another watching the door, she was satisfied that now was her best opportunity to get to work on the car.

Lucy didn't break her stride. She looked inside her handbag, located her purse and unzipped the coin section. She let the purse fall, spilling loose change on the ground, next to the subject vehicle. Dropping quickly to crouch, she placed her handbag at the rear offside wheel, gathering some coins with one hand while feeling underneath the car with the other. The place where she had expected to find the old device was empty. She knew that it was definitely still attached but she couldn't locate it. 'Come on!' she told herself, quickly restarting a fingertip search. Time was running out. She couldn't afford to be noticed by any shoppers or by a bored CCTV operator in an office somewhere. Moving a fraction further back, she found it, removed it and stowed it in her bag with one fluid movement. Then she attached the new device in her preferred position. She picked up the last errant coin, placed it in her purse, grabbed her handbag, stood up and walked away towards the shops at a leisurely pace. She felt elated but kept her face stoney. Sending a series of clicks, she communicated with Kelly, letting her and the team know that she had been successful. It felt great and it lifted the energy of the whole team.

Lucy bought herself and Kelly a takeaway coffee, returning with them to the squad car, allowing Kelly to head out. Kelly promised to return before her coffee went cold. Lucy sipped her drink, hearing that Kelly had entered the shop. An operative inside the shop alerted her that the subject and his girlfriend were making their way towards the tills. Kelly could see them. They were loud and easy to spot, standing in an open area towards the front of the shop. She assumed that the bloke she could see shopping on the mezzanine floor was the operative, since his location gave a bird's-eye view of the entire store. She was reassured to see that he looked natural and he attracted no attention.

It appeared to Kelly that the subject and his girlfriend were having some sort of disagreement over the purchase of a hideous-looking ornament. She browsed a rail of t-shirts watching as hand gestures and shoulder shrugs abated and they walked together towards the checkout. She picked up a t-shirt and followed them. Kelly stood behind the pair, queuing to pay for her purchase, and watched the subject produce two different bank cards from the pocket of his tracksuit trousers, along with some cash. While the cashier rang up a new pair of trousers and the ornament, he peeled some notes from the bundle in his hand.

Pity, thought Kelly who had hoped he'd use a card to pay. Happily, his girlfriend leaned closer to him, nuzzled at his neck and said something Kelly couldn't hear. He shrugged her off in weak protest, but then handed most of the cash to her. As she tucked it inside the cup of her bra, he handed over a black bank card to the cashier with a flourish. Kelly smiled to herself as they walked past her, the subject's girlfriend swinging a carrier bag. She stepped forward and paid for her own purchase, which served to mark the subject's transaction, took her time to pocket the receipt and left the shop.

Rejoining Lucy in the car, Kelly buckled her seatbelt and reached for the still-warm cup of coffee.

'Told you!' she said, taking a mouthful.

'A present for you,' Kelly said, unfolding a white t-shirt emblazoned with Enjoy your Trip and a smiley face.

Lucy laughed and they grinned all the way back to the office for the debrief.

The Geordie DI could scarcely believe what the team had managed to achieve in such a short time.

'Canny job! I thought we'd be at it for at least a week.'

'We don't mess about,' Kelly told him, signing off paperwork.

'I take it you won't be driving back up tonight?'

'No, I think we've covered enough miles today. We're staying the night in a hotel, which according to your lot, is in the shady side of town. We're all going to have a meal and a beer together tonight. Lucy and I will travel back up tomorrow after a full English.'

'Decent. If either of youse fancy a job here, just let us know. An' I mean that.'

Pulling up at their hotel, Lucy parked as close to the front door as she could, in the only area of the car park which was overlooked by a CCTV camera.

'There's a good chance we'll be the victims of crime here, so leave nothing in it. Unfortunately, no self-respecting criminal would want to take our car away, so we'll still have no working stereo on the way home,' Lucy said.

'If I had seen the state of this hotel first, I would have done the job even quicker,' Kelly said wrinkling her nose.

Before they had even had a chance to check in, Lucy's work phone rang. It was Inchy and he was ecstatic. It was a long time since she'd heard him so happy. His opposite number at the National had already called him to pass on his thanks and Inchy was basking joyfully in the recognition.

Closing the door of her hotel room, Lucy switched on her own phone. She had reverted to leaving it switched off again. Danny was still pestering her with texts and the regular buzzing of incoming messages was more than she could stand. By choosing when to switch it on she felt slightly more in control. She left it switched off overnight now since his late-night and middle-of-the-night messages had managed to disturb the short periods of sleep she managed between nightmares. Every time she looked at her phone her heart sank, and her stomach twisted. If she didn't need it to keep in touch with her friends and family, she would gladly throw it away. Sure enough, as soon as it had sprung back into life, it buzzed like an angry wasp as a series of text messages rolled in. Reading through them, she saw that her mum had sent a couple, just checking in. Lucy smiled as she read the properly spelled-out words, excellent grammar and abundance of emojis. Her smile froze then disappeared as she read the messages from Danny. They followed the pattern she had become so familiar with: declarations of love, that he missed her and that he couldn't live without her. Then they became sharp, asking why she wouldn't just reply to let him know that she was alright, Was that too much to ask? Had she forgotten him so quickly? Had she moved on? Who was she spending so much time with now that she couldn't even give him the time of day? It was draining. The last few were darker with brooding, threatening content.

If you don't contact me in the next hour I'll do something silly.

I can't go on.

How could you do this to me?

Who do you think you are?

You're nothing special.

You're a fucking nobody.

You're a fucking slag.

She was a slut, a whore … and then her eyes widened as she read the last, which told her to watch her back, and said chillingly, *I will kill you and nobody will care.*

Lucy sagged, sitting on the bed as she read. It was relentless. Tears of frustration blurred her eyes. She wanted to reply, to tell him to leave her alone, but she knew that would be even worse than just ignoring him. It would only fuel the fire of whatever drove him.

She had been hungry on the drive to the hotel, but she had lost her appetite now.

20.

The success of the Manchester job was quickly forgotten when Lucy returned to her own office. She had noticed that her DS, Chris Summers, was a little quieter than usual and it felt like he was avoiding her. She wondered if it was because he expected her to take up the job she had been offered with the national team and would leave his squad for the bright lights down south. He had nothing to fear on that score, she was happy where she was. As she pondered this, Chris stuck his head round the muster room door, looking for her.

'Lucy, a word, please?'

'Yes,' she smiled back, getting up and locking her computer.

Lucy found Chris in Inchy's office, where the pair were deep in hushed conversation. Knocking on the open door frame, she walked in, and the men silenced.

'Shut the door,' Inchy told her, sounding ominous and failing to make eye contact.

'Hope I'm not in trouble,' Lucy said smiling, but with a creeping feeling that she might be. She racked her brain for anything she might have done to land herself in his bad books but came up with nothing. The atmosphere was serious enough for her to start worrying that something bad might have happened to her parents. Looking for clues, Lucy's eyes fell on Inchy's desk where she immediately recognised her own handwriting and wished the ground would open up and swallow her. She was staring at the notebook she had been keeping which logged all of Danny's nuisance text messages and calls. Oh no! No, no, no. They had both read it and now the cat was out of the bag.

'What's this?' Inchy asked her. Not waiting for a reply, he continued, 'How long has this been going on?' He hardly paused before asking, 'Who knows about this?'

Jesus, thought Lucy, still reeling from the discovery and now unable to keep up with his round of quick-fire questions. He must have been bottom of the class on the Detective Officer training course when it came to interviewing suspects. He fidgeted in his seat, awkward, uncomfortable and out of his depth. His voice had a hard edge of self-preservation to it. Lucy imagined that he was already trying to work out how this situation might adversely affect his own career prospects. Before she could arrange her thoughts and say anything in reply, Chris filled the gap by telling her that he was sorry, he couldn't keep quiet and had felt compelled to make the boss aware.

While Lucy had been away, Chris had been looking for a phone number connected to Operation Flame. He had let himself into her locked cabinet, rifled through her drawer and had stumbled across her private notebook.

This is not what was meant to happen, Lucy thought. She had been convinced it was safe there. Her cheeks flamed hot with embarrassment and exposure. She didn't want to discuss it, particularly not with Inchy, who lacked tact and empathy, and who now looked like he might be about to have some sort of medical episode. He tugged at the already loose collar of his shirt. He was sweating and his red face matched hers. She could plainly see that he would rather the discovery had not been made and was already working out how he would explain it to command.

'How long has this been going on?' Inchy asked again, meeting her eyes for the first time.

Lucy wondered how little she could get away with disclosing. She watched her hands twisting in her lap, mortified to be having the discussion and worried about the now, very real possibility of Danny losing his job if a police investigation was launched. She was acutely aware that he was the breadwinner for his family. It wouldn't be fair for them to be without his wage. She reasoned that even if she told them everything, it could go no further without her making a formal complaint, so maybe she could give just enough information for them to make him stop contacting her and they could leave it at that?

'Not long,' she answered.

Lucy was certain now that she had been correct about her job in the squad being at risk. It felt like she was about to be let go. Inchy rubbed his ruddy face with his hands and puffed his cheeks out, as if about to say something difficult. She felt sick. A ringing noise started in her ears as she thought about how unjust it was. She hadn't done anything wrong; she hadn't even come forward to report it and now she was going to lose her job in the agency.

She was tired of covering up the nuisance calls, the messages – all the unwanted contact. It was exhausting and it made her quiet and withdrawn. Her social life had completely ground to a halt. Even when she did have time to meet her friends or have a family meal, she made excuses and stayed away. She was keeping secrets from the people she loved most, and it was easier to do it from a distance. She was so tired from the nightmares and a lack of sleep that she ended up spending her time off staring blankly at the television screen with the sound down, unable to concentrate and without enough energy to do anything else.

Juggling all these thoughts, Lucy was jolted back to the present when Inchy resumed his questioning.

'How long were you together? When did you start seeing each other?'

Lucy looked at him, knowing that he didn't care about her, and that he had no interest in what might happen to her or her career. In his eyes she was merely a problem. It was her fault, she had landed in an unexpected situation; he had been unaware that she and Danny had even been in a relationship. It hadn't been a secret, but he had missed it, caught up in his own world. Now he was annoyed.

'We lived together for a while, but it didn't work out,' Lucy said resignedly. 'Ask me anything you want.'

Her stomach rolled and churned, growling audibly, she hadn't eaten anything yet that day. Her clothes had become loose on her already slight frame. She had only noticed when she had to use a safety pin to hold up a pair of trousers which used to be a snug fit. Her collar bones had become more visible and her hip bones protruded. Under their scrutiny, she felt smaller and more vulnerable by the second, she pressed her knees with her hands to stop herself from shaking.

Inchy's mouth was a thin, tight line as he tapped his pen testily on her notebook. Chris's face was pale. She saw that there were dark circles under his eyes and genuine concern in them. He said nothing because he didn't know what to say. He had no idea she had been going through such a hard time, she'd kept it all in and she hadn't dropped the ball. He was sorry to have missed the signs. He saw now that she was stooped and skinny. Her cheeks were hollow, and it looked like she had been missing sleep. He had noticed an increase in the amount of phone messages and had seen her leave calls unanswered, but had dismissed it, imagining it was just an indication of a busy social life. Now he thought about it, he had been close to telling her off about the phone, as it had been irritating and not what he expected from her.

'Where's your phone?' Chris asked her.

'In my bag.'

'Can you get it for me?'

Lucy got up reluctantly, went to her own desk and retrieved her bag. She could hear the chatter of her oblivious colleagues, but they felt distant, even when she was in the same room. She went to hand her mobile phone to Chris, paused, taking it back and switching it on before placing it in his waiting hand. As soon as the screen came to life, texts began to drop in. She could guess who the sender was. Only three texts arrived from Danny, thankfully fewer than she would have expected for the time of day. Chris's cheeks flushed as he opened and read the first message. He keenly felt the invasion of her privacy and decided he had seen enough – there was no need to go through the rest. Asking why she had made the log, he handed back the phone.

She answered honestly, in a small voice, 'Because I thought that if he killed me, you would eventually find the book and know that it was him.'

She had been determined not to cry, but heat built up inside her from saying the words out loud, and caused a single tear to escape and run down her cheek until she caught it with the back of her hand. Smearing it and blinking hard to stop any more, she felt alone and sad.

'Jesus,' Chris said, under his breath and looking at Inchy, who blew out air from pursed lips.

'Why didn't you report it?' Chris asked.

'I didn't want to get him into trouble,' she said, feeling childish.

'Right.' Inchy closed the book and looked even more awkward. 'I'll hold on to this. You go back through. In fact, why don't you go home?'

'I'm okay,' she said, sniffing.

She knew that the offer of an early finish was not for her welfare, but to get her out of the way, so that he could call the bosses and work out what to do with her and the information they now had.

Lucy stood up, wiped her nose and trudged miserably back to her desk. She would keep her head down. It was bad enough that the bosses knew, but she couldn't face the humiliation of the rest of the office finding out.

On the drive home, Lucy's left leg started to jiggle nervously and she felt lost. She didn't want to be alone in the flat but didn't want company either. Without conscious consideration, she went back to the flat, packed a bag and headed to the gym. Picking a treadmill away from anyone else, and which faced the door, she began to run off some of the nervous energy and worry.

After the session, Lucy showered, making sure that she only closed her eyes for the shortest time while shampoo ran down her face. Talking about Danny had made him loom larger in her mind and placed her back in a state of high alert. What if they'd already spoken to him? Let him know he was in trouble? He might be after her right now, to shut her up for good. Walking the short distance from the exit to her car, Lucy kept her eyes up, scanning the area all around her. He wasn't there but she expected to see him. Her heart stopped for a second, when she thought she'd spotted his face behind the wheel of a car.

Stopping at the local shop on her way home, Lucy walked round, picking up her usual pint of milk and fresh bread, still looking for Danny in the faces of other shoppers and checking the door every time it opened. She hurried home, spooked and not wanting to be out in the open any longer.

Checking inside her flat, she was satisfied that he hadn't been there in her absence. She loaded the washing machine, reviewing the day's awkward meeting in her head, blushing deeply with a wave of fresh humiliation. Then she wondered what Danny would do if she was brave enough to officially report him to the police, to make a criminal complaint against him. Rubbing sweaty palms on her trouser legs, Lucy's heart rate increased, and she looked unconsciously towards the front door, knowing that he would be absolutely livid with her and would become a much bigger threat. There was no way she could give a statement against him and lodge a formal complaint. It was already clear that Inchy found the situation distasteful, and she was sure that the commander wouldn't think twice about booting her out of the agency if it would hush up anything unpleasant. Her mind was made up – definitely no formal complaint. Lucy was tired, but restless. She reached under the kitchen sink, grabbed the bucket containing cleaning products, threw in a bottle of bleach spray and began to clean the already spotless flat from top to bottom.

Finally, she moved around, carrying out her regular bedtime routine, checking each window and the door, making sure the little early warning traps were set. Then she climbed into bed, physically and emotionally shattered. Her eyes were gritty but wouldn't close, running over the ceiling instead. Rubbing her face, Lucy smelled the cleaning products she had used still clinging to her skin. She yawned widely, hoping for sleep but dreading the nightmares which lurked.

21.

As usual, Lucy was first to arrive at work the next morning. She looked at her mobile. Danny had only sent four messages overnight. Maybe he was finally losing interest after all. If there was a chance that the messages and calls would cease, then perhaps she could ask Inchy not to say anything at all to Danny, to leave it as it was. Before she could decide whether or not to start a new notebook, loud chatter in the corridor announced Roddy's arrival with a couple of the others. Closing her desk drawer, she chewed absent-mindedly on a nail as Roddy clattered about, opening and closing his own desk drawers, conducting a search.

'Aha!' he said, holding aloft the mug which proclaimed, Number 1 Dad. 'Here, you,' Roddy said, waving the heavily stained mug in Lucy's direction, 'Why's the kettle not on? Is it broken?'

Lucy rolled her eyes at him.

By the time DS Chris Summers walked into the muster room for the day's briefing, everyone had a mug of tea or coffee in front of them.

Lucy sat straight in her chair, a notepad and pen at the ready. She was surprised that Chris had not caught up with her to share any new information or to let her know there was none, before the team briefing. Trying not to read anything into it and not letting disappointment register on her face, Lucy listened as he went on to tell them that from the Manchester connection, they had solid information that a large cocaine consignment destined for Operation Flame, was expected to arrive at Aberdeen harbour.

The Aitchison clan were further out of pocket thanks to a couple of well-timed drugs warrants being executed and a respectable amount of cocaine being recovered. It was enough to have a couple of their gang remanded in jail, awaiting trial. Ralph Aitchison had been incandescent with rage when he learned of the loss. It was lucky for the two that they had gone to prison to wait, delaying them having to face Ralph and explain what had gone wrong. He could have their punishment doled out in prison if he wanted but he was too busy trying to recoup some of the loss. As well as the drugs, the police had seized £20,000 of cash under the Proceeds of Crime Act.

In Ralph's youth, the police could be bought. If they had seized his money back in the day, there was no way that the full £20,000 would have made it back to the Drug Squad office. Before it was photographed and lodged it would have shrunk. They might even have taken a bit of the Charlie, but they were never too greedy. They would keep some for themselves, lodge some to keep their bosses happy and leave him with the rest. He could afford the old 'tax' on his business. He didn't care for the modern police force, which was far too clean for his liking. Ralph Aitchison didn't like to admit that he was missing Lee. He had no time for his flash swagger – the permanently present, obnoxious cloud of aftershave got right up his nose. Lee made silly mistakes, showing off his wealth in the wrong places, but he was handy to have around. Ralph was finding it increasingly hard running the club and the drugs business by himself, which was how he had managed to give those two clowns too much responsibility and they had messed up. Maybe if Lee had been there, the police wouldn't be sitting on his drugs and his cash. Ralph thought bitterly that he should be doing less at his age, not more.

He had bags under his eyes and was permanently tired. He felt his age. The last stint in prison had been no picnic, even with the extra privileges and comforts he had paid for. His prison sentence had been for tax evasion in relation to the club. He had laughed when they had charged him after a long round of police and HMRC interviews. They couldn't get him for attempted murder, drug-dealing or even assault charges, but they got him on taxes. He'd stopped laughing in prison. He hated thinking back to it, all the noise, the constant shouting, howling, banging, clanging and crying. If he closed his eyes, he could still smell the distinctive, fetid aroma of disinfectant, musky body odour and stinking, unwashed feet. It remained with him, even in his office at the club when he was practically choking on Lee's bloody expensive aftershave. He never wanted to go back to jail. He didn't have it in him to do another stretch.

It was time for him to get out of the game, to retire. Somewhere warm, but not too hot, with decent fishing in a country with no extradition laws. The trouble was that those countries felt too far away from home and what he knew. He'd been to Spain twice. He didn't like it and hadn't bothered going away on holiday again. He doubted that he'd be able to find somewhere with a decent cup of tea and a full Scottish, or even English breakfast, in the kind of places he'd been considering. The police were really starting to get on his nerves. It made him angry to think that at this rate he would never be able to buy his dream home somewhere in the Scottish Highlands, on a good game-fishing beat, and have enough money to keep him for the rest of his days.

He noticed that his retirement fantasies never included his wife, Mary. She annoyed him even more than the filth. He reluctantly tolerated her extravagant spending and stupid, cackling friends. Her family wouldn't stand for divorce. They were deeply religious, which he thought was ironic, since they were among the biggest bunch of criminals in the UK. Nowadays, all that remained of her gangster father was a shell. He'd been put out to pasture in some eye-wateringly expensive old folks' home, not knowing if it was New Year or New York. When he went into decline, the family business had been handed on. His daughter, Mary, had not been considered to take over the business. She hadn't even been allowed to run the almost-legitimate front, which was their roofing business, far less the drugs side. The old man's god was not an advocate of women's rights, so the business had been handed over to Mary's brother John.

John was a nasty piece of work, even from Ralph's skewed perspective. *Pure evil* is how Ralph thought of him. He'd heard everything about John before they had even met, through their mutual business interest of drug-dealing. Ralph had never really liked the violent side of their world. He tried to avoid it and kept his hands clean as far as possible. Once he'd established a reputation it had been easy to keep, using others on his payroll to dole out the beatings and punishments. When Ralph had been rising through the ranks, starting to make a name for himself and being taken seriously in the underworld, he'd been noticed by John who encouraged him to go out with his sister. Ralph had been flattered by the attention and the respect from John, not from Mary. He was sure he could do better than Mary on the looks front, and she was no cook, but he'd learned pretty quickly that this was no romance, it was the coming together of two empires. Joining forces allowed them to share the wealth and neither man stepped on the other's toes. There was no need to spill blood or go to war over boundaries and territories.

Ralph suspected that Mary had been as reticent as he had been for their union, but even she couldn't go against her family and the deal had been done. Ralph closed his ears to rumours that she was unfaithful. He had paid for tennis lessons, but when the chatter about Mary's affair with her trainer had become too loud, he had an associate visit the young man, who had been encouraged to relocate his business abroad. Mary had been furious, refusing to speak to Ralph and for months after the tennis pro left, she punished him by spending with extra abandon and treating her freeloading friends to all sorts of luxuries. When she had taken up with her life coach, Ralph had laughed in her face. He hadn't even needed to sort him out. John had surprised him by insisting on fixing that problem himself. The man had simply disappeared. Years later, when Ralph and John had been drinking together, John confided that he had taken the man fishing. They had been several miles offshore when John took a meat cleaver to him and fed him to the fish. Ralph believed him. He feared John even more than he loathed him. He was a complete psychopath with an appetite for bloodletting. Ralph felt increasingly trapped in his own life. He wanted out.

Ralph hatched a plot for one last, big deal, planning to keep the money for himself and disappear. With Lee still missing in action, he couldn't wait any longer. The club was running at a loss and the other side of his business needed an injection of cash. Ralph cut out his usual intermediary and took a trip to Amsterdam by himself, arranging for the importation of £1 million worth of cocaine. Refinancing his house had covered half the cost. Then he'd sold every piece of Mary's jewellery that he could get his hands on. She'd handed it over to him willingly, buying his story about a safety deposit box to keep it hidden away from the plod. She had even handed over £100,000 in cash. He had been shocked to find that she had obviously been keeping a secret stash of money and how much she had accumulated. The rest had come from John.

Ralph had hated asking for it. Since he couldn't share his plan nor afford to split the spoils, he'd told him that he needed it to pay off a woman. John had enjoyed hearing that. He had a glint in his malevolent eyes as he handed over the cash and slapped him on the back a little too hard.

The drugs were due to arrive in Aberdeen harbour along with some legitimate cargo. He had to rely on the Dutchman's word that it would be well concealed. He had assured Ralph that it would stand up to scrutiny, but sensing his greenness, he offered a tip, telling Ralph to have a unit ready to receive his package, somewhere it wouldn't look out of place and would give an air of legitimacy. Ralph rented a lockup in what he thought was a quiet industrial estate. Unfortunately, his neighbours had been too welcoming and a little too curious about the new enterprise next to them. They had smelt a rat, and unbeknown to Ralph, the police were already on to him.

In the squad's muster room, Lucy listened carefully to the update from Chris Summers. She was gutted that it had been kept from her. Even worse, was the omission of her name when Chris had tasked the team, directing a recce of the industrial unit. Her cheeks flushed with frustration, but she said nothing publicly, waiting until he had finished and the team were scrambling together their equipment before she asked to speak to him. Sheepishly, Chris told her what she had already guessed. She was being kept out of the field and had been placed on administration duties, confined to the office, effectively left out of her own drugs operation, just as things were beginning to develop after several long months of work. Feeling defeated and willing herself not to cry bitter tears, Lucy logged onto the computer. It stung, but she resolved to throw herself into the back-office side of Operation Flame, she would still work hard. Fishing out telephone records, she resigned herself to a headache of a day, sifting through the data dump, looking for evidence relating to the new industrial unit and the importation.

22.

Sitting at her desk, using an empty coffee mug as a paperweight, Lucy squinted at her computer monitor, matching numbers to the print in front of her. Highlighter pen in hand, she scrolled down lists, marking the sheet as if she was playing a game of bingo. Her eyes were slow to focus. She leaned back in her chair, rubbed her eyes, rolled her neck and looked about. The office was quiet. Most of the team were out tailing one of Ralph Aitchison's men. A handful remained at his new industrial unit, scoping it out, finding suitable vantage points and plotting the surrounding area.

Adding to her annoyance, Lucy's phone vibrated in her pocket. Checking the screen, she saw Danny's number, cancelled the notification and shoved it back in her pocket. Hadn't she blanked him for long enough for him to get the message and move on by now? She could hardly remember the old days, what it felt like to receive a text or call from him and be excited. Every notification these days, gave her a sense of dread and left a heavy stone in her stomach. Heat built inside her, anger overtook annoyance, making her restless. She felt excluded at work, paying the price for the ill-fated relationship, which was exactly why she hadn't reported it in the first place. Why couldn't he just leave her alone? Lucy tossed the highlighter pen on her paperwork, agitated, glad to see that she was only sharing the room with an analyst who was engrossed in her own work. She got up, needing to move about, to blow off some steam and stop feeling sorry for herself. She didn't want to cry in the office, especially when she was trying to convince Chris and Inchy that they should deploy her again. As she contemplated making another cup of coffee, Chris Summers stuck his head round the door. With a sideways glance at the analyst, he nodded to Lucy, saying nothing but indicating that she should follow him. She was glad to leave the desk behind, following him through the corridor. Chris avoided eye contact. *Not again*, she thought.

'Someone wants a word,' he said, pointing to the door of Inchy's office which was ajar.

She couldn't see inside the room and when she turned back to ask Chris who it was, she found that he had already gone. He'd melted away back into his own office, the door closing softly behind him.

Walking into the detective inspector's office, Lucy could smell the lingering scent of dog from his old jacket, indicating that he had been here recently, but he was nowhere to be seen now. Sitting in his place was an unsmiling woman of about 40, wearing a navy suit and a grave expression. Her straw-coloured hair was pulled back in a tight ponytail and she smelled of shampoo. She offered no introduction or explanation, but had made herself quite at home behind Inchy's desk. In contrast to her cool demeanour, a younger man dressed in a tight-fitting, dark-grey suit, sprang eagerly to his feet. His hair was gelled firmly into place and didn't move as he bounded towards Lucy, thrusting out his hand in greeting and offering a wide smile. Lucy looked into his eyes and saw uncertainty. He grabbed Lucy's hand clumsily, then almost tripped over his own feet as he scrambled to pull a chair into place. He smelled so strongly of cologne that she regretted having shaken his hand, knowing that the headache-inducing, woody fragrance was bound to remain on her skin. She unconsciously wiped her hand on her trouser leg. He hung his jacket over the back of the chair closest to the woman, leaving Lucy the third chair with its back to the door, facing her.

Ah, thought Lucy, *classic police interview set-up*. So, this was their game. The too-eager man who had moved about the small space like an ungainly Labrador offered Lucy a glass of water. As he rose to get one, she declined the offer and he stood, statue-like, momentarily unsure of what to do next before sitting back down again. He had a strong Glaswegian accent – not a local, then. Without being told, Lucy guessed that they were from the Professional Standards Department and that they must have been drafted in to glean as much information as possible from Lucy and report back to the big bosses. Lucy's stomach had already dropped and now it started to churn with unease. Wishing she had eaten a more fortifying breakfast than two Rich Tea biscuits and three cups of coffee, she sat down and placed her hands on her knees to stop her legs from tell-tale shaking.

The Labrador introduced himself as Detective Inspector Ian Dobson. His unsmiling colleague was introduced as Superintendent Jeanie Forbes. As anticipated, they were from Professional Standards or the 'rubber heelers' as they were known. Lucy eyed them with suspicion, reflecting their mistrust of her.

'Where's my DI?' she asked.

'He's working from another office for now,' the superintendent told her in a clipped, formal voice, which still held a Glasgow accent but was easier to understand. That figures, Lucy thought, *what a coward*. He hadn't even had the decency to tell her that this pair were going to pay her a visit, let alone offer any kind of support. Chris had scurried off to hide in his office too. It looked like she was on her own now, she had obviously been dropped by her supervisors.

Lucy considered that the two suits before her were an awkward paring, they gave her the impression that they didn't usually work together. She did not recognise either of them and wondered if they knew Danny, or he knew them. Maybe they were already on his side, they were certainly not on hers. From the frosty start, she suspected that the superintendent had already made her mind up about Lucy before they had even met. She looked at the superintendent's ring finger, and saw a gold wedding band and a thin gold ring with a diamond on it. They looked well-worn, suggesting that she had been married for a while. Looking more closely at her finely-lined face, Lucy guessed that she was about 45 years old. There was a worn Mulberry handbag on the desk next to her. She wore no make-up and although her clothes looked to be good quality, they were not fashionable. The overall impression was of an austere, no-nonsense person. Lucy couldn't imagine that the super had much of a life away from her work.

Lucy's head began a dull thud as she sat in the cramped and airless office, realising that they would be in it for the long haul. The Labrador pulled out a black faux-leather, A4 folder from a briefcase, placing the folder on the desk in front of him. From their behaviour and the interview style set-up, she had half-expected him to whip out a *suspect* interview form.

Wasting no time, the super flattened her notebook with one hand, a heavy-weight quality pen in the other, and without looking at Lucy, asked in a toneless voice, 'Full name?'

Good grief, Lucy thought, *not even a rapport stage first?*

Lucy balled her hands in her lap, gave her full name, her date and place of birth and her address to the super, as the Labrador scratched the same details on a blank page.

Tired of waiting to be told what was happening, Lucy asked, 'Why am I here?'.

The super eyed her cooly and replied, 'You have made an allegation about a fellow police officer. We are investigating that allegation.'

Lucy's eyes widened. 'No, I didn't. I have made no allegation or complaint.'

The super sighed audibly, waved her pen and told Lucy, 'We need a formal statement from you.'

Lucy gave a thin smile, shook her head slowly and decided that she wouldn't be providing them with any further information. She had no desire to share the most secret details of her personal life with them. She was being treated worse than a criminal. At least they didn't have to ask what was going on. She didn't want to speak to them, but she couldn't afford to make enemies of them either. If they had treated her like an adult at the beginning or even given the reason for their visit, she would have been able to tell them that she had nothing to say and would have saved them from wasting any more time. Lucy took a deep breath and politely explained that there was nothing she wanted to discuss with them and apologised for their wasted journey. Instantly, the mood in the room shifted. The Labrador had, until then, been overly attentive, leaning towards her with a smile which didn't reach his eyes, but now he looked disbelievingly between Lucy and his super, his face as vacant as the statement page before him.

The super bristled in Inchy's chair causing it to creak under her shifting weight. Her eyes narrowed in her pale face as she regarded Lucy with displeasure. Lucy swallowed hard. She snapped, 'We'll see about that.'

The super swivelled her pen closed, replacing it and her notebook inside her handbag. Then she turned to the Labrador who, under her withering stare, had managed to look even more dog-like, resembling a scolded one with its ears held flat against its head. At her nod, he rose to his feet and opened the door. Lucy's cue to leave. She left the office hoping that their paths would never cross again. As she returned to her own desk, her mobile phone vibrated ominously in her trouser pocket, making her feel that she was stuck between a rock and a hard place.

23.

After a sleepless night, Lucy returned to work at her usual early time, and was dismayed to see an unfamiliar, unmarked police car parked outside the office.

'Damn!' she muttered under her breath. She steeled herself as she entered the building, hoping that she might be wrong, but expecting to have another encounter with the charmless pair of rubber heelers.

Before she had even climbed the stairs, Inchy's angry red face appeared above her, peering over the banister. *Not good*, Lucy thought. She hadn't even managed to shed her jacket before Inchy escorted her back into his airless office. Already seated at his desk, and in the same formation were the two Professional Standards officers. Inchy stood with his hands on his hips, fizzing with annoyance as he told Lucy that she was not allowed to remain silent on the matter of Danny; she was in fact, duty-bound to cooperate with their enquiry. Lucy took a step back, her throat constricted. She couldn't quite believe what he was saying.

'But as the partner – or rather the *former* partner – of the person being investigated, I can't be forced to be a witness, to give evidence against him.'

She saw a vein pulse in Inchy's temple, and his eyes bulged. He worked his mouth, but he was at a loss – it seemed he had forgotten this part of criminal law. The superintendent, leaned forward on Inchy's chair, and pushed a photocopied page of text across the desk towards Lucy, turning it for her to read. The super pointed to a highlighted paragraph of slightly blurred text. Saving her the trouble of reading, she was told that she was correct, in 'normal' circumstances she would not be a compellable witness, however, as a serving police officer, that right did not apply to her. She added that the text had been copied from the Police Regulations Act and reinforced that Lucy could not remain silent, she was duty-bound to comply with their enquiry. Lucy felt a wave of nausea grip her, she might as well have trotted out the old police cliché, 'There's an easy way to do this, and there's a hard way.' There was no mistaking the implied threat, it was no longer just her future career in the squad at stake, now they were threatening her job in the police force. Lucy slumped down into the 'interviewee' chair, cornered and resigned to discuss the most intimate, most cripplingly embarrassing parts of her life with stony strangers. At least Inchy had slid away.

'Let's start again,' said Ian Dobson, opening his folder.

Lucy took a deep breath, and let it out slowly, steadying herself. *Okay*, she thought, *if you want it, here goes, the whole mess.*

An hour into the statement which felt more like an interview, Lucy could tell that they were genuinely shocked by her revelations. Several times as she recounted events, she had been distracted by the super anxiously tugging at the collar of her blouse, in discomfort. Ian's eyes had widened, and he kept looking at the super for reassurance, as if he was fighting to stop himself from asking her, 'Can you believe this?' Lucy saw in their reactions that her disclosure was far more serious and brutal than they had anticipated, and they weren't even at the worst part yet.

Lucy looked at the super. She saw someone who lived a straightforward, ordinary life, who was unable to imagine how anyone, far less a police officer, could find themselves the victim of domestic abuse. Lucy imagined that when she had been assigned the enquiry, she had wrongly assumed that Lucy had engaged in an affair of some kind, with a man who had ultimately rejected her, causing her to seek revenge with some made-up stories.

The superintendent produced a buff cardboard folder, removing Lucy's notebook log from inside it. Tucked into the pages were sheets of paper, printouts from Lucy's mobile service provider. Several lines were highlighted. She was asked to give her own mobile telephone number and to confirm that the records in front of her related to her phone. Lucy's saw hundreds of lines, shocked afresh to see the large volume of them, grouped together. She was led through some particular entries, asked for clarification and to provide some background details.

They broke for lunch. As Lucy moved to stand, the super and Ian exchanged meaningful glances and she was asked to remain where she was. The Labrador was dispatched to retrieve sandwiches and drinks for them all. They would remain together in Inchy's office for a cosy dine-in lunch. Lucy closed her eyes and puffed out her cheeks, realising that it was being done to keep her away from her colleagues. The duo would want to speak to them before Lucy could, just in case she primed them. *Good luck if you're looking for intelligence there*, she thought, picturing Roddy's gormless face. The Labrador walked towards the door, still looking back at Lucy and the super, confirming the lunch order as he opened the door, barging straight into Roddy, who had been standing outside the door, trying to eavesdrop. Lucy rolled her eyes – amateur effort, considering his day job.

Later that day, Lucy sat feeling wrung-out. She was shattered and had a splitting headache despite washing down paracetamol tablets with her tuna sandwich at lunchtime. She had gone through gruelling details of the assaults in minute detail, until she had become distressed. Panic engulfed her, making her dizzy and she could hear the woosh of blood in her ears. She had given up trying to hold herself together, unable to keep her composure or to care what they thought of her any more. Ian went to fetch water while Lucy sat with her head between her knees, the dirty carpet swirling before her eyes, trying to regain control of her senses. As she sipped lukewarm water from a chipped mug, her eyes met the super's and for the briefest of moments, saw a human reaction.

Later, the super asked Lucy to explain why she had failed to report any of the crimes. Her shoulders sagged and she told her truthfully, 'I was ashamed. I haven't told my family. My closest friend doesn't even know exactly how bad it is,' Lucy said, wiping a hand over her dry mouth.

The super studied cobwebs in the corner of the ceiling, gathering her thoughts before telling Lucy, 'I spoke to your dad. He was upset.'

With that, the last of Lucy's defences tumbled down. She hadn't expected them to speak to her parents, but of course it would have been so easy for them to catch her dad at work. They would have wanted to know if she had told him or if he had seen anything to corroborate or rule out an allegation of domestic abuse. To see if she was lying, she realised. She hated the thought of him finding out in such a harsh way from tactless strangers. The thought that he would be upset intensified her own distress. The super told Lucy what she had already guessed, that they had paid Chief Inspector Russell a visit at his office after Lucy had failed to divulge any details the previous day. Her father hadn't contacted Lucy afterwards, agreeing to wait until they had noted her statement. She imagined that he would have slept as poorly as she had last night, after that bombshell.

'I'll need your phone,' the super told her.

'But all my contacts are on it ...' Lucy hated the phone but felt bound to it, needing it for contact with the friends and family she was keeping at arm's length.

The super examined Lucy's face, firmly but not unkindly, she told her, 'You have a job phone. You can use it until you get your own one back. I'll give you time to transfer any numbers you need.'

Lucy sat, juggling the two phones on her lap. She struggled to focus under their watch, hastily adding contact names and numbers to her work mobile phone. When she'd finished, she placed her mobile into the 'hamster box' – the small, specially designed brown cardboard box with a clear plastic window which would house her phone until it was forensically examined.

'Take anything you want from it. I have no secrets now and nothing to hide,' Lucy told them.

'I know,' said the super, tapping on the pages of her mobile phone records still lying on the desk.

Lucy wiped her nose on the back of her hand, all self-consciousness gone. She checked the wall clock while the super and her colleague packed away their things. Seven o'clock. She needed to visit her parents now. She had a lot of explaining and reassuring to do.

'Any questions?' asked Ian, zipping closed his folder.

'No, but please let me know when you're going to speak to Danny.' Lucy asked.

'Why?'

'He'll be really angry and I'll need to be ready'.

'Yeah, of course.' He waved his hand dismissively.

Lucy hoped he would keep his word.

By the time they were finished for the day, everyone else in the office had already gone home and Lucy felt more alone than ever.

24.

After the exhausting day she had spent in Inchy's office with Professional Standards' finest, Lucy had visited her parents and had the most awkward conversation of her life with them. Her mother had been completely floored, her father hadn't forewarned her, deciding to delay the hurt and spare her feelings until they could all sit down together. He had had time for the initial shock to wear off, allowing him to remain composed during their family meeting, supporting his wife and daughter. The news had been utterly staggering to him, coming from nowhere and had been made all the worse when he thought of her suffering alone. After too many tears and cups of tea, Ruth and Ian Russell wanted Lucy to remain under their roof where they could be sure she was safe. Lucy had insisted on going back to the flat, anxious to maintain her routine as much as possible, to process her own thoughts and keep at least a sense of normality. They had fed her, hugged her tightly and reluctantly waved her off. Lucy had felt slightly better after the visit, feeling a little lighter with the heavy secret lifted. It was liberating to have finally got everything out in the open.

Lucy didn't miss the millstone of her mobile phone. It had been a relief to drop it in the evidence box. The first message she received on her work phone was from Inchy, suggesting she use some of the abundant annual leave she had accrued but never taken. It would suit him to have her out of the way, it would save him and her colleagues any awkwardness while the enquiry was conducted, since they would potentially end up as witnesses in the case. Lucy had assured him that she didn't need any time off and that she'd be back in the office as usual. She had asked if he might find time for a chat but heard nothing back. She knew that he would hate the thought of a face-to-face conversation with her, but she needed to know where she stood, and he couldn't hide away forever.

Now she lay in bed, unable to sleep. Her mind turned over different scenarios of Danny being confronted by Professional Standards. He'd be livid. She could only guess how he would react but was sure she would be the target of his ire. They would probably tell him to refrain from contacting her, the usual patter, but goosebumps crept over her skin, knowing that he was likely to pay no heed to that, he'd do what he liked. He would know that he had to be clever about it, but she doubted it would stop him. She wondered how many of the silent calls and vile texts she had received from new, anonymous numbers the enquiry team would actually be able to attribute to him. Yawning, Lucy wondered how long it would be until they got hold of him and in the meantime, how many messages were still arriving as her phone lay in a production store somewhere, miles away from her. The nastiest messages were usually sent late at night, no doubt after he had been drinking. She shuddered, picturing him full of hatred and blind violence. She hoped the enquiry team would get hold of him sooner rather than later. The suspense was already awful. She had to accept that it might take a while, that they would carry out further investigation, building a case against him before they brought him in for questioning. They'd been unable or unwilling to give her any timescale, so all Lucy could do was hope they wouldn't take long. Then she would have to prepare herself for the fallout after they let him go.

The next morning, Lucy walked towards her desk, coffee in hand, to find that a few of the squad were already seated at their desks for an early start which she had not been privy to. The office was suspiciously quiet, the low hum of conversation eerily at odds with the usual loud morning scrummage. She had obviously been the topic of conversation judging by the sheepish looks on the faces of her team and their sudden silence. Lucy tried her best to ignore the quiet. She looked at a newspaper which had been left on her desk. It was dated from the previous day and the pages had been folded back to show a particular article. Placing the mug on her desk, Lucy picked up the newspaper and saw that the piece was about healthy eating. In bold type, the subheading read, 'Tendency to bruise easily? Eat these foods to help'. Lucy's cheeks flamed as she put it down again. If the paper had been left as a joke it wasn't a funny one.

She avoided eye contact with her colleagues, concentrating more than was necessary while logging on to the computer. Trying to maintain a nonchalant air, she wondered which one of them had left it. She felt thoroughly miserable, in a place where she had thrived until recently. She had no time for them now, wishing that they would all get out of the office and on to the plot as soon as possible. It hurt to be kept out of the loop for Operation Flame, having no update on the recce of Ralph Aitchison's new industrial unit. She would just have to grow thicker skin. She rubbed knuckles over her lips, thinking how she had been pushed around by Danny, her DI and the rubber heelers. Now her own colleagues, some of whom, until now she would have considered friends were turning their back on her. She was just an uncomfortable presence in the office, a pariah.

Sick of feeling overlooked, Lucy locked the computer, got up and walked out the office. There was no sign of Inchy, he was obviously still dodging her, but she could phone him. She'd had enough. Lucy walked purposefully to the toilets, shut herself in a cubicle and sat down to dial his number. Unsurprisingly the DI didn't answer her call. She sat in the dim, pine-scented space, looking at the phone in her hand. *Think, Lucy! Come on*, she told herself. He wasn't a clever man; he was a coward, and a fully paid-up member of the CID boys' club. What would he do next? She felt keenly that he wanted her out of the way and ideally out of the squad, an attempt to separate her from the agency and prevent its name being next to hers on the chief constable's briefing paper, or even worse, in the newspapers. She hadn't wanted to make an official complaint; it was he who had started the ball rolling.

Lucy thought about the newspaper left on her desk. She was certain that it wouldn't be long before the story was leaked or fed to the press. The media would probably have a field day. She screwed her eyes tightly shut, imagining what sensational spin they would put on it. She didn't want her name to appear on news feeds or in papers that her family and people they knew might see. She felt sick at the thought, recalling that one of the last things the super from Professional Standards had said to Lucy as they packed up to leave, was that she must not talk to the press. At the time she'd been stunned by the comment. The super had seen the expression on Lucy's face and told her that it would be 'inevitable' that there would be media attention. Until then, it hadn't even occurred to Lucy, but on reflection, a police officer being charged with domestic violence, breach of the peace, stalking, offences against the Telecommunications Act and anything else that they could evidence, would obviously be of interest to the media.

Since she, the other person involved, was also a police officer, they would be all over it. She couldn't bring herself to use the term 'victim' when referring to herself, even in her own head. Cursing under her breath, she realised that her troubles were far from being over.

Lucy pocketed the phone and splashed cold water on her face, bracing herself for the walk back into her office. With steely resolve she looked at her reflection, she was damned if she'd just roll over and ask for a transfer out of the department. She determined that she would remain there at least until the whole circus concluded.

25.

More days had passed in an office stalemate for Lucy and with no news from the Professional Standards Department. Lucy assumed that this meant that they hadn't yet caught up with Danny, but at least he seemed to have stopped sending messages to her work phone. She had become resigned to her solitary administration role in the office. She felt less alone after a couple of the team had reached out to her, letting her know that they cared, but she was all too aware that they had not done so publicly, feeling the weight of peer pressure.

Kelly had sent a slightly rude joke, which she had followed up with a text saying that she hoped the rubber heelers would find it funny when they read it. Lucy had smiled at the small but significant gesture.

Lucy could hear Inchy's voice. He was back in his office. She rose from her desk; they needed to have a chat. Lucy knocked softly on his door which was open anyway. The DI looked up, seeing her and gesturing to an empty seat. He sat back in his own chair, a sad smile on his face. Small talk was not his strong suit, so Lucy went first.

'Boss, I need to be back out with the rest of the team. Things are picking up with Operation Flame and I want to be in the thick of it, not stuck in the office. There's only so much I can do there and I've already run out of work.'

'Lucy, you're on light duties. You're under a huge amount of stress and I can't let you make a mistake which could hurt you.'

'But I won't.' She leaned forward in her seat, palms up.

He sucked in air, steepled his fingers and looked at the desk. 'They're not letting you drive anymore.'

Lucy sat back again, momentarily stunned. 'Why?'

'Stress.' He spoke quietly.

Her eyes blazed, 'I'm not suffering from stress.' But as the words left her mouth, she heard a hardness to them and saw him react, to slightly withdraw.

'It's not up for discussion, Lucy.'

They sat in silence for a beat. Long enough for her to realise that there was no room for movement. She had to accept that if she wanted to remain in the squad, she would be stuck in the admin role indefinitely.

'Why don't you take a little time off?'

She smiled weakly, nodded and left his office, not trusting herself to say anything else.

Lost in thought, sitting back at her desk in the empty office, Lucy jumped in fright when a set of keys clattered on the corridor floor next to the open door, followed by swearing in an accent she instantly recognised as belonging to DI Ian Dobson, from Professional Standards. Lucy felt a headache develop just looking at him. Her stomach dropped. He didn't need to say anything. She logged off the computer, gathered her belongings, grabbed her coat, and followed him along the corridor to Inchy's office. The DI stood, shouldering on his jacket, getting ready to leave. Ousted from his office again. He gave Lucy another sad smile and patted her arm on his way out. Superintendent Jeanie Forbes entered the small office, sat on Inchy's still warm chair.

Lucy's eyed the freshly opened box of tissues which the super placed at the centre of the desk. This did not bode well. She doubted they were intended for anyone else other than her. Looking from them to the super's face, Lucy knew that whatever lay ahead was expected to be traumatic for her. Her pulse quickened and her palms began to sweat in response.

No greetings were exchanged before the super got straight down to business. Ian assumed his role as scribe, copying Lucy's details from her statement. She noticed that it had been typed up and highlighted in places. She tried to read the marginalia, to prepare herself and work out what they wanted to discuss. There was no indication. In her wildest dreams, Lucy could not have imagined that the super's first words to her would be, 'Do you enjoy rough sex?'

Lucy's mouth fell open, her eyes bulged and she looked at the super, trying to work out where on earth this had come from and where it was going. In the silence that followed, Lucy closed her mouth, and looked at Ian for any clues. He met her eyes and she registered with disgust a slight smile on his lips.

'It's an easy enough question. Do you?' He asked coolly.

'What?' Lucy asked, confused.

'Do you like rough sex?' the super asked again.

'No!' Lucy said, appalled and embarrassed.

'DS Rae told us that you do,' she said.

Lucy's mind raced, her heartbeat rapid and shallow, she felt dizzy, at once realising that they had spoken to him, and that they had failed to give her the early warning that was promised. A chill ran through her body, her face burned bright with embarrassment.

'You spoke to him.' Lucy said, incredulous.

She should have known better than to trust their word, but she was still surprised and felt let down. Silence hung thick and heavy in the air. She hoped to god that neither of these two were unleashed on the public, on 'real' victims. Lucy forced herself to get a grip. A boxer, swayed by a low blow, she needed to find strength to look after herself, to fight her corner. She had been rocked, but now she was finding her feet again.

'What exactly does that have to do with anything?' Lucy met the super's gaze and steadily returned it.

Before she could answer, Lucy had already worked out what must have happened. She assumed that Danny would not have been picked up by them, not treated like a criminal. Instead, he had probably been invited to a police station on a voluntary basis, for 'a word'. At least it would have spared his long-suffering wife and children from further humiliation, she thought. Once in police custody, he would have been told what they were investigating and what the allegations against him were. From there he would have been offered access to a duty solicitor at no cost to himself, possibly even one provided by the Police Federation. That solicitor would have reaffirmed to Danny that he should keep his mouth shut and provide a 'no comment' interview by answering every question with those two words. The solicitor probably even reminded Danny of the most basic defence available to an allegation of domestic assault where the victim bears marks of violence – rough sex. A vile thing to allege, heaping further shame.

Anger burned brightly in Lucy. She felt it for herself and on behalf of every other person who had been abused and who had managed to find the courage to report the crimes against them, only to suffer the indignity of the salacious accusation; a smear and unspoken judgement on their character. Anyone who did want to engage in, or who enjoyed rough sex was welcome to it, but they probably wouldn't wish the fact to be broadcast to all and sundry by being disclosed in a court case. Lucy had worked on a murder case where the only person alive, who truly knew what had happened, was the accused. He had denied the crime and had been perfectly willing to have his dead partner, the mother of his child, called 'kinky' and 'perverse' in a court trial, with her grieving family forced to listen and endure the falsehood, as the murderer tried to save his own skin at the expense of the victim's reputation. This, Lucy realised, was absolutely no different. The gloves were well and truly off now. Danny was fighting for his home, his job and his liberty after all. She had automatically assumed that he would follow the mantra of, 'Deny, deny, deny', but had not actually considered that he would play dirty, or how low he might be prepared to stoop. She knew the answer to the question she had asked the super, but she wanted her to say the words, for some sort of acknowledgement that this was bogus.

Lucy would not allow herself to look weak again in front of them. With her hands clenched, she dug nails into the palms of her hands, willing herself to stay strong, unblinking, waiting for an answer.

'That is what he alleges,' she replied evenly. 'You told us that you were in a romantic relationship with DS Rae.'

'I was,' Lucy replied.

'DS Rae denies this,' the super said.

Lucy's mouth fell open again, an involuntary chuckle escaping. This was getting crazier by the minute. She wondered why he would deny this most basic fact. Then she supposed that this would also form part of his defence, by refuting that they had been in a romantic relationship, he was not disputing that they had sexual relations, just saying that they had not been in a romantic partnership. He was attempting to further discredit her good character by suggesting that she engaged in indiscriminate sexual contact, probably with anyone who crossed her path. He was able to reach her through the rubber heelers and knew it would sting Lucy to be dismissed like this. It lit a fire in her now from the smouldering flame of injustice. *Okay*, she thought, *let's go*.

Drawing herself up in the chair, Lucy took a steadying breath, then in a clear, measured voice, told them, 'We lived together, we had a joint tenancy agreement, a joint bank account, even a joint gym membership. I am still in the process of removing him from all of them.'

As Ian struggled to keep up the transcript, Lucy slowed her words, ensuring that they would be accurately recorded. She picked up her handbag and removed her purse, pulling out a card.

'When you had him in custody, and forgot to let me know, did you search him? Were his personal possessions taken from him and logged?'

The pair exchanged uncomfortable looks, which Lucy took to be a negative response.

'If you had, you would be able to check the custody sheet, listing his possessions. I'm sure his bank card and gym card would have been recorded,' Lucy continued.

She carefully placed her own joint account bank card and gym membership cards on the desk, turning them so that Ian could write their details.

'We still have a joint gym membership at a place close to the flat we used to share. I still pay the £68 monthly subscription. We agreed to a year's membership which I am trying to terminate,' Lucy told them.

Lucy looked at the super, who gave only the slightest of nods. She was hard work but there it was, the first crack in her facade. With that tiny gesture, Lucy knew that the super didn't believe Danny. She had seen right through him, but she'd had to give him a fair opportunity to set out his defence. A serious allegation had been made against him which carried with it a potential prison sentence. She knew that Lucy was telling the truth, but she needed to prove it beyond all reasonable doubt and to shoot down Danny's defence.

Lucy went on. 'The content of his text messages to me should also suggest more than a casual relationship. We discussed purchasing a house together, child care and I arranged and paid for repairs and servicing to his car.'

Lucy collected her cards, put them away, folded her arms and sat back in the chair. She could have gone on, but she felt weak as a wave of adrenalin left her. She was not convinced they could be trusted to carry out a decent investigation.

After the rubber heelers were satisfied that they had covered the points they needed to, the addendum statement was zipped away in Ian's folder, and they packed up again.

'One more thing,' Lucy halted them. 'Did you get an interim interdict?'

Already doubting their capabilities, she had asked them to seek the formal document during their last meeting but heard nothing back. She knew that a piece of paper wouldn't save her life, but hoped that it might help end Danny's pestering, thinking that being served the legal document might finally bring him to his senses. It would also offer her slight comfort, knowing that should he breach the terms by contacting her again or turning up at her flat, he could be immediately arrested.

'No,' said Ian, squeezing a bulging file into his briefcase and checking his ridiculously large wristwatch. 'It was decided an interdict would not be necessary in this case.' He looked up and fixed her with a patronising smile.

'*Interim* interdict,' Lucy corrected him, not sure he knew the difference, or that he even cared.

Lucy opened her mouth, ready to correct him, but she closed it again. She felt there was no point in wasting any more energy on him. She determined to look after herself. As Roddy was fond of saying, 'Crime fighters? They couldn't even fight sleep.' Lucy was about to leave when the super addressed her.

'Lucy,' she said, peering into her handbag, 'the press has got hold of the story.'

26.

As Lucy left Inchy's office after her latest encounter with the charmless pair from Professional Standards she met DS Chris Summers. He looked awkward for just a beat but recovered and enquired if she was alright. Accepting his offer of a coffee, they sat down together in his office. Lucy asked about Operation Flame, what stage it was at now and how they were set-up at the industrial unit.

'Not bad at all,' Chris told her, between sips of hot coffee. 'We have vision and sound. Pretty much just waiting for the nod from the port now, so don't worry too much about the phone stuff.'

'Okay,' she told him. 'I'm through it all anyway.'

Chris Summers regarded her over the rim of his coffee mug.

'What are you going to do?' he asked.

'I'm staying here if that's what you mean. I'm not going to walk off into the sunset.'

'What's happening?' he asked her.

'Well, I believe you have already had the pleasure of meeting Professional Standards' finest. I don't feel reassured,' she told him, balancing a mug on her knee and moving it in circles, attempting to do the job of the missing office teaspoon, dissolving coffee granules.

'Do you think he'll hurt you again?' Chris asked.

'Yes. I wouldn't be worried otherwise. What do you think?'

'I think he's a real and credible threat. The agency trained him to break into cars and houses for a living and he certainly seems to have lost the plot.'

'Yes, and now I've threatened his job and his freedom. He was angry before, so god only knows what he's like now. They didn't even bother to get an interim interdict.'

'What? I'd have assumed that was a given?'

'Apparently not.'

'Still staying in that flat by yourself?'

'Yes. I'm still tied to the lease for a while yet and I'm stubborn. I don't want to have to move back in with my folks.'

Chris put his mug down, picked up the desk phone and dialled.

'Stay here,' he told her, pushing a pad of Post-it notes towards her while looking for a pen. Producing it and handing it to Lucy, he said, 'Write down your address.'

She did so as his call connected, and he spoke to the police control room inspector. Within ten minutes, Chris had arranged for a marker to be placed on Lucy's address. It would lie dormant in the police emergency system unless anyone called to report suspicious activity or a crime in progress. Then the marker would ping and the controllers would be alerted that there was a potentially violent domestic crime in progress, with a life at stake. He also arranged for a community officer to meet Lucy at her flat, so that it could be fitted with a wireless system, connected to an alarm. She would be issued with a handheld, panic alarm linked to the same system. If activated, a radio message would automatically sound over all the police radio channels with an individual code, identifying the location, ensuring a fast response. Lucy felt slightly relieved. At least her fears were being recognised and taken seriously.

'Lastly,' Chris said, turning to face her, 'have you seen Occupational Health yet?'

'No,' she blushed, 'I don't think I need to. I'm managing fine by myself.'

'Maybe you are just now, but what happens if you can't? What if it does become too much?'

Lucy considered this. She was past the point of risking any career damage by asking for help with her emotional wellbeing. She knew the ship that was her surveillance career, had already sailed. She could not cause any more damage to her professional reputation or career by admitting that she was living on her nerves. Covering her mouth, she let out a yawn. It seemed that she had an almost constant headache and was permanently tired these days.

'Well, maybe they could help me sleep,' she conceded grudgingly.

'I'm sure they can. Make an appointment,' he told her. 'I can do it for you if you like, but if you self-refer there is less the agency can find out, if you know what I mean,' he told her, looking towards the door to ensure that he was not being overheard. 'If the job refers you, they can ask specific questions. If you put yourself forward, there's less feed back. You're meeting the community cops at your flat in an hour, but you've got enough time to phone Occ. Health for an appointment first.'

With that, he left his own office, closing the door behind him, so that she might have privacy to make the call. Lucy stared hard at the desk phone. Then she took a deep breath and picked up the receiver.

27.

Lucy believed that she was coping well when she had made the call to Occupational Health. But when it was answered by a kindly receptionist, she had surprised them both by breaking into uncontrollable sobs as soon as she had begun to explain the circumstances that had led her to make the call. The receptionist had been lovely, reassuring Lucy that she was okay, making sure she had privacy, but wasn't alone. Then she had coached Lucy, helping her to regain control of her breathing, before giving her clear instructions to follow. She told her to sit still for five minutes, then, when she was ready, she had to visit the ladies' toilet, where she could wash her face and compose herself before fetching a glass of water, returning with it to Chris' office, where she should wait by the phone to receive a call back from a member of medical staff. Lucy did exactly as she had been told.

The following afternoon, Lucy found herself seated in one of the eight chairs which lined a corridor. She was alone in the makeshift waiting area and sat nervously. Her bare forearms kept sticking to the plastic coated, wipe-clean fabric of the chair, making her feel even more uncomfortable. Anxiety had built up in Lucy from the moment she had been referred to the 'Nutty Professor' by Occupational

Health. She had convinced herself that the psychiatrist would be in cahoots with the police force and would report back that she was insane. She would be discredited and required to resign her post, allowing the whole matter to be conveniently swept under the carpet. Her worries had increased severalfold with the realisation that the location for her appointment, 'Rose Garden', was in fact, a ward in the psychiatric hospital.

She arrived early and had passed several uneasy minutes sitting in her car at the hospital car park, scanning around her to ensure that she had not been followed by a newspaper reporter and that Danny wasn't lurking nearby. She'd watched patients and staff come and go while she considered leaving. It had taken a huge effort for Lucy to finally enter the hospital, walking with leaden feet to the reception desk and then to the waiting area. Now she sat, eyeing the door which led to the exit.

Before she could leave, a man in his fifties, wearing an honest but slightly worn navy-blue suit, walked towards her. He had springy grey curls, soft blue eyes and a reassuring smile.

'Lucy?' he asked. 'Hello, I'm Malcolm Davidson.'

Lucy managed a tight smile, then followed him along the corridor to a large light and airy office.

Professor Malcolm Davidson, Principal Adviser to the Police Force and mental-health expert, took his seat behind a vast wooden desk. As she'd driven to the hospital, Lucy had told herself that she would be positive when dealing with medical staff, but remain wary. However, within ten minutes of meeting the professor, she felt she was in safe hands. He was disarmingly caring and professional.

She liked him, finding the process much less frightening than she had anticipated. He asked Lucy what she considered her greatest anxiety was, at that moment. When she had confessed that she genuinely feared that he might have her sectioned under the Mental Health Act, he had cracked up, laughing even more when she admitted that his nickname at the agency was the 'Nutty Professor'. He'd written it on his pad, chuckling and telling her that he would be delighted to share that information with his wife and his colleagues.

After two hours, Lucy left the hospital. Although her head was pounding, she felt better. She had been completely open and honest when answering the professor's questions and had almost wept with relief when he had told her in a matter-of-fact way that she was not going insane, and that she would get better, that the sleeplessness and anxiety would eventually pass. The nightmares and night terrors were symptomatic of the trauma she was dealing with. If she allowed herself to accept some help and gave it time, she would recover and sleep soundly again. When the professor had left his office for a few minutes to call a colleague to arrange some counselling for Lucy, she had not been able to resist the urge to check the notes that he had made. Stretching forward over the desk, she read with difficulty, his upside-down handwriting. It looked like a series of squiggles, but she was able to decipher some words and phrases before he returned: *PTSD, risk-taker, classic overachiever with a low boredom threshold.*

She didn't doubt that the professor was an extremely clever man, he was an expert in his field, but she had been shocked that he'd diagnosed Post Traumatic Stress Disorder. Lucy was unsure exactly what it was, and what it meant. He told her that it was a common condition, and that after what she had experienced, and in her line of work, he would have been surprised if she had not developed it. She didn't expect to meet the professor again, she would be dealing with his colleagues in the future, but she was sure she'd never forget him and would be forever grateful for his help.

28.

Lucy had taken up her parents' offer to stay at their house for the weekend. She had been happy to be away from the flat for a few days and understood they had wanted to ensure she was alright, to keep an eye on her. She knew that in their eyes she was a 31-year-old child. Eating her mother's home-cooked meals would do them both good. Fiona had telephoned to check in with Lucy. She had agreed to call round at Fiona's first, on the way to her parents. Fiona wanted to catch up properly.

Lucy and Fiona sat together with cups of tea in front of them on a table, forgotten and cooling. Lucy had felt sheepish when she sat down with Fiona, guilty for not being able to confide in her after the last assault. Apologies tumbled from Lucy's mouth, Fiona quietened her with a hug, telling her that she had nothing to be sorry about. Lucy tried to explain how embarrassed and foolish she had felt, going back to him after everything she had already gone through.

She told Fiona about the enquiry, giving a short, humourless laugh as she recounted her experience with the super and the Labrador. Telling her that they had door-stopped her unsuspecting father at his police office, asking him if he was aware that his daughter was the victim of domestic assault and stalking. She told Fiona that they had not been so much 'rubber heelers', more like 'steel toe-cappers'.

Fiona bit her lip and told Lucy they had paid her a visit at work too. At least when they had called at Fiona's office, she had already been aware of the first assault, and that Danny had been calling Lucy and sending unwanted text messages. She had still been shocked to discover the full extent when they had told her. When they had asked if she knew about the latest assault, she had shaken her head, deeply saddened to think of her friend being brutally attacked. She had been appalled by the pair's lack of personal awareness, finding them to be insensitive and had told them as much. In Fiona's job in the Public Protection Unit, she headed challenging enquiries involving abuse, violence and sexual offences, many committed against children and vulnerable people. Many of the adult victims she dealt with had suffered at the hands of an abuser for years before they finally found the strength to speak up. She had told the indelicate pair that she hoped they had used a little more consideration and compassion when they had spoken to her friend. Now she wanted to educate them again after Lucy described her dealings with them.

As they sat chatting, Lucy's phone rang. They both looked at the screen in Lucy's hand, checking to see the caller ID.

'If it's him, pass the phone to me. I'll deal with it,' Fiona said, tight lipped.

It wasn't Danny, but Lucy's mother, Ruth. Answering the call, Lucy heard an artificial brightness in her mother's voice which immediately rang alarm bells. She stood up, listening with growing concern, as her mother told her that something suspicious had just happened. She had been at home alone, when a woman had called round, casually asking if Lucy was in. She had assumed that the friendly woman on her doorstep must be a friend of Lucy's or a colleague. As she spoke, the woman looked past Ruth, searching as much of the house as she could see, paying close attention to the framed family photographs which hung on the walls. She answered the questions, letting her know Lucy was out but was expected home in time for dinner. Then she became suspicious. When she asked if she could come in and wait, Ruth hesitated, realising uncomfortably, that this woman was a stranger. She thought quickly, telling her that she was just about to leave for the afternoon, and asked the woman what her name was.

'Sarah,' she replied, taking longer than necessary to answer such a simple question.

Ruth decided to probe, to find out whether she was genuine or not. Testing her, she had remained outwardly friendly and had asked if she knew Lucy from her school days. When she said that they had attended secondary school together, Ruth had made up a fictional school name.

'Oh, Saint Stephen's?' she asked.

When the woman had smiled and nodded, Ruth had added some made-up school friends just to be sure.

'You must know Marian and Morag Kindness then?' she asked.

Ruth's intuition was right. Her suspicions were confirmed when the woman had fallen into her trap, answering her with a confident, 'Yes, that's right.'

Ruth offered to take a message, and her contact details so that Lucy could call her when she returned home, but she declined, made her excuses and left. Ruth waved her off, noting the details of her car and its registration number.

'Lucy, I think she's a journalist. I honestly didn't expect them to turn up at the door and I didn't think they'd be sneaky, pretending to be your friend.'

Sitting back down again, and feeling hot with annoyance, Lucy was sure that when the registration number was checked on the police national computer, it would be owned by a journalist or media company. Lucy reassured her mother that she hadn't been foolish at all. She had done well, thinking on her feet.

Lucy felt crushed. The last thing she wanted to do was cause her parents any more grief. She was frustrated to think that the haven of her parents' home had been breached.

The reporter who had visited Ruth knew that the police wouldn't allow Lucy to speak to her, but had hoped to glean any snippet of information to go with the piece she had already written. She was intrigued that a police officer was the victim of domestic abuse, she wanted to see Lucy with her own eyes, to judge her and to understand how it could have happened, especially when the perpetrator was another police officer. The public would want detail.

They wanted a photograph of Lucy to run with the article. Ideally, she would have a black eye or at least be looking downcast – a good 'victim' snap. They had already bagged a photograph of an angry-looking Danny, as he answered his front door and unleashed a volley of expletives to the reporter and photographer. They had been reliably informed by an 'unnamed source, close to the pair' that there was an 'angry wife' in the house too, but unfortunately, she hadn't come to the door, not even when they had shouted her name. *Never mind*, the journalist thought, as she drove back to her office, *they still had a chance to snap a photograph of Lucy*. A photographer crouched in the back of a small van across the street from Ruth's home, waiting for Lucy to return.

Lucy apologised to her mother, telling her that she would miss their planned dinner. It'd be better for her to stay away just now, but she promised to keep in touch.

'Keep an eye out, Mum. Let me know if anyone else bothers you,' Lucy told her, ending the call and staring at her phone in resignation.

'Why don't you stay at mine?' Fiona offered. 'They won't come here, and heaven help them if they do.'

'Thanks, that's really kind, but I don't want to.' Lucy sighed. 'I'm fed up with scurrying about, hiding and living in fear. The last thing I need is a photograph of my face and for my name to appear in the paper. That would give the agency all the ammunition they need to move me out. There's no way I could carry on then, it would be an easy end to my surveillance career.'

Lucy wished for a quiet life, one where she was able to come and go as she pleased, where she didn't feel hunted by Danny or by the press.

'I'll get us another cuppa,' Fiona told her. 'I'm going to order a pizza for us too. Sorry it's not your mum's cooking, but it'll have to do.'

Fiona wandered off to the kitchen, placing a hand on Lucy's shoulder as she walked past, and was horrified to see Lucy recoil from the slight touch, still on alert.

'Sorry, Lucy.'

'No, no. It's okay. I just can't help it,' Lucy told her.

A few minutes later, Fiona walked back into the living room, making sure that Lucy heard her approach and careful to stay in front of her, where she could see her. She had plenty of experience in dealing with victims of domestic abuse, and she found herself unconsciously slipping back into work mode.

'Right! Good news,' she told Lucy. 'A Mighty Mega Meat Feast pizza is on the way. The kettle is on, and my auntie

Kathy has had a cancellation next week for her holiday home. How about taking some of the leave they're so keen for you to use and going to Tiree for a break?'

Lucy sat forward, rubbing her face with her hands. She hadn't wanted to take time off, but she was surplus to requirements at the office, and now journalists were circling her flat and her parents' home. They would probably stake out her office too. Then there was the dreadful thought of Danny paying her a visit. Even the Nutty Professor had told her that she could do with some time away from work, and she believed that at least he had said it with her best interests at heart.

'I'll call Chris. I'm sure he'll happily do without me, and if it's okay with Kathy, I would love to take her up on the offer,' Lucy said, remembering the beautiful scenery and fresh air.

'Great,' Fiona beamed, slapping her hands on her thighs. 'That's settled then. Take my car from here. We can swap. No doubt some of the people you want to avoid will already know what you drive, but they won't be looking for my car.'

Lucy nodded her head in agreement.

'I'm sure there were journalists pulling into the street when I left for work today,' Lucy told Fiona, remembering the male driver and a female passenger, probably the same 'Sarah' who had visited her mother, now that she thought about it.

29.

DS Chris Summers immediately agreed to Lucy's proposal of taking a couple of weeks off, using up some of her annual leave. He sounded genuinely pleased when she had told him that she had met the Nutty Professor and that she had found him very helpful. She told him about the probable journalist who had visited her mother and he asked her to wait while he checked it out. He confirmed the car was registered to a national newspaper group. Lucy looked online and recognised one of their staff journalists as being the female passenger in the car she had passed on her way to work, probably the same one who had visited her mother.

There had been no sign of anyone hanging around her flat when she had returned to it and she hadn't been followed there, so she tried to put it out of her mind as she packed for a couple of weeks holiday on the island of Tiree. The flat felt even more inhospitable now, not helped by Lucy keeping the lights off while she moved around, emptying milk cartons and gathering the kitchen bin bag to dispose of it. The smell of overripe fruit led her to a small bowl on the dining table in her living room. She tipped the browning apples and bananas into the bin bag, then moved to the side of a large living-room window. The blinds were angled to prevent anyone from seeing inside, but allowed her the sliver of a view. With nothing to be seen outside, she looked around the sodium-lit room where she stood. The place brought her no joy now, and she looked forward to the day when her lease ended, and she could hand back the keys to the agent. Two weeks away from this gloomy prison would do her good.

Lucy walked into the kitchen, seeing the black box of technology which sat on the counter, left behind by local police officers. The alarm was primed and ready to shout a code over the radio of every police officer in the area if it was tripped. Despite its presence, she still set her own traps round her flat, making sure that every window and door was covered.

Lucy picked up her phone – still using her work one – with no idea when she would ever be reunited with her own one. She was in no hurry to have it back. She had already decided that she would sign a disclaimer, allowing the police to dispose of it when they had finished with it. She would replace it with one which was physically different, and ensure that even the ringtone was new. She plugged the mains charger into her mobile, set the alarm for the early start she needed to catch the ferry, then settled into bed. It was late again, and she was exhausted. Her eyes nipped. Puffy bags lived underneath them. She pressed the heels of her hands into her eyes, seeking relief but only seeing stars.

The next morning, as soon as the ferry had pushed off from the mainland, Lucy stood on the deck, deeply inhaling sea air. She felt better already. She had held back when it had been time to board, wanting to be the last vehicle so that she could scan the faces of each foot passenger and peer through vehicle windows, looking for Danny's face or anyone who might be a journalist. She watched every passenger, noticing their behaviour, discounting groups of smiling faces which she easily identified as tourists. She saw that most of the solo travellers wore blander expressions. Their movements were efficient and unprompted, suggesting that they were frequent users of the service, probably locals. When she was finally satisfied that no hack hid among them, Lucy allowed herself to relax.

Lucy had been instructed to drive herself to Kathy's house where she had to move a certain flowerpot and help herself to the 'bothy' key. The newly installed guest accommodation in Kathy's garden had obviously been reclassified from 'pod' to 'bothy'.

On the drive there, Lucy had kept checking her rear-view mirror until the road behind her emptied and she was alone and able to enjoy the scenery. By the time she had unpacked her bags and placed her walking boots and flip-flops by the door she felt brighter. An air of quiet calm hung around the place. It was cosy and cheerful, smelling of fresh, new wood. Kathy had left a pint of milk in the fridge with some butter. A small hamper sat on the table and held a bottle of wine, a packet of handmade shortbread biscuits, a jar of bramble jam, an assortment of teabags, a pack of ground coffee, a pretty mug and a sourdough loaf. The sun was high in the sky, the weather typically breezy, but warm enough to explore the shoreline in her shorts and a t-shirt. Lucy didn't bother with her flip-flops, stepping through open doors, onto the small area of decking and down steps on to the cool, pale sand. Her bare feet found purchase as the sand shifted under her weight, propelling her towards the sparkling sea.

Gulls cried overhead and Lucy squinted against the bright sun to focus on them as they circled higher and higher. The salty, seaweed air clung to her nostrils, soothing her troubles and her sore head. She felt her body still, finding peace, and realised that this was what she had been missing. Lucy felt as if every molecule in her body had finally stopped rushing about, slowing to let her muscles unclench. The fog and tunnel vision which had clouded her brain was beginning to clear. This was a safe place. The tiny hamlet of houses around Kathy's home was a tight-knit community. Anyone new here would be instantly recognised as such. There was nowhere to hide. Lucy felt instinctively that she would sleep well, hoping to rest properly, to galvanise herself and be ready for whatever lay ahead.

Walking back to the bothy with a sheen of sweat on her forehead, Lucy struggled to focus, looking at the shadowy front steps of the bothy. The contrast between bright sunshine and dark made it difficult to see, but there was something there which had not been present when she left. As she got closer, she saw a sheet of white paper held under a smooth stone. The edges of the paper, exposed to the breeze, flapped and danced. Lucy felt a sudden wave of nausea. Her heart began to hammer, her breathing became jagged. She felt weak and dizzy, as if her legs might fold under the weight of her body.

Somebody knew she was here, and they had been at the bothy while she was out.

Lucy's eyes darted about the few low lying, scrubby bushes near to the bothy. None were big enough to conceal an adult, but she looked for Danny in them anyway. There was no sign of movement beyond the bothy towards the quiet little street and its row of cottages.

Get a grip! She urged herself, trying to rationalise what she was seeing against what she felt. She was unable to listen to her own advice, overwhelmed by a sudden, uncontrollable emotional storm.

Lucy fell to her knees in the sand, clutching the paper, panic stricken and tearful. Her heart rate had increased to the point where she thought she might be having a heart attack. Shallow, panting breaths made her feel light-headed and that her lungs couldn't get enough air. Her vision closed in, tunnel-like, and her ears rang. The noise of the wind, the waves, and the gulls fell away, becoming muffled as if she was under water.

Lucy became aware of movement to her left, from the side of the bothy. Someone was approaching but she couldn't get up, couldn't flee, she was a statue.

'Lucy! Lucy!' Kathy shouted, running to her side. She crouched down, gently stroking her back. In a soft, calm voice, Kathy gave words of reassurance, telling her over and over again, that she was okay.

'Breathe with me. Deep breath in, two, three. Hold it now. Slowly let it out, two, three, four.' Kathy repeated and Lucy followed her instruction.

Gradually, Lucy felt her senses return. Blinking away tears, she felt embarrassed and small. She apologised, saying, 'I thought it was from him.'

'Oh, you poor thing. You've nothing to be sorry about.' Taking the paper from Lucy's hand, she said, 'This is a note from me, inviting you to the house for coffee. I only popped back to leave another, telling you that I've made some cake for us.' Kathy waved another piece of paper.

Lucy smiled through tears, hiccupping and wiping her face with the stretched arm of her t-shirt.

Smiling at her, Kathy said, 'This is what I call *sea-mail*. Very different to email. It's much nicer'.

Lucy's breathing steadied as she calmed.

'You're okay,' Kathy told her, smoothing Lucy's hair away from her face. 'Just a wee panic attack'.

'Good grief,' said Lucy, 'I thought I was going to die.'

Lucy shook her head at herself. *This isn't right*. She decided to call the counsellor she had been referred to by the Nutty Professor. It was time to accept some help, she certainly couldn't live like this.

30.

Robbie Gillies sighed as he hefted a gym bag over his shoulder, freeing a hand to search his pocket for the front-door key to his flat. Not so long ago, he had been pleased to call this place his home, and enjoyed the impressed look on people's faces when he gave his address. It surprised him how quickly he seemed to have descended into a life where violence, drugs and threats were commonplace. It was far removed from his old, low-paid labouring job, but he would gladly take that back now; he would give his right arm and possibly more if he could swap his life back to how it used to be. He would happily give up the flat to sleep soundly under his mother's roof in his childhood bedroom.

Every time he slotted the key into the lock of his front door, he held his breath. Ever since he had cooperated with the police, letting them bug his flat, he couldn't settle. He was acutely aware that unseen ears were listening in to his life. People he would never meet knew how he spent his waking hours and how long he slept. They knew when he broke wind, what he watched on television and the music he played. They heard the rustle of sweet wrappers and takeaway cartons and knew how poor his diet was. He tried to make himself behave as normally as possible, but he rarely forgot he was in a goldfish bowl.

When he was forced to entertain, Robbie felt the presence of the bugging devices even more keenly. He felt so ill at ease that he became clumsy, wooden and unnatural whenever an associate dropped round. He was amazed they never seemed to notice. He cringed while they casually discussed sex, violence and drugs. They even took drugs while he glanced guiltily around. Robbie thought back to when he was growing up and how he had wanted excitement in his life. He reckoned that he had accumulated a lifetime's worth of it now. Sighing, Robbie unlocked the door and stepped into the dark hallway of his flat, dropping his bag on the floor and lumbering towards the light of his large open-plan kitchen and lounge area.

Absent-mindedly, Robbie opened a kitchen cabinet, grabbed a pint glass and turned on the cold-water tap, letting it run for a few seconds before holding the glass under the stream. The sound of someone noisily clearing their throat, only a few feet away from where he stood, caused Robbie to jump in surprise. The glass dropped into the sink, it hit the unyielding stone basin and shattered, the noise startling him all over again. Spinning round, Robbie automatically balled his hands into fists, facing his visitor.

'Lee!' Robbie exclaimed.

His heart was still hammering as he dropped his hands to his side, opening and closing his mouth vacantly under Lee Aitchison's glassy gaze. Lee regarded him with a half-smile on his face. He had enjoyed sneaking into the flat, planning how he would surprise Robbie. He had been disappointed to find that Robbie was out when he arrived, but he had waited patiently and had been rewarded with a reaction which was even better than he had hoped for. Now he saw Robbie squirm under the magnifying glass of his stare, he was satisfied. He had been hiding in the shadows for too long, where nobody had given him the automatic respect he commanded on his own patch, cowering before him. He had missed this, the feeling of being alpha dog, feeding off fear and eyes downcast, not able to meet his own.

'Hello, son.' Lee said. It was his usual greeting to Robbie, even though they were similar in age. Robbie recovered his composure, gathering from this familiar, small exchange that Lee meant him no harm, and that he obviously had no idea about the covert devices planted in the flat. He forced himself to smile and controlled his breathing. Lee got to his feet, gesturing towards him with an empty whisky tumbler that he wanted more. He waited to be served by Robbie, even though the bottle of Johnnie Walker Blue Label sat next to the chair he had occupied. Lee waited for Robbie to walk over and pour him a drink. Robbie saw no other glasses and assumed that Lee had been alone in the flat, drinking by himself. He tried not to show his annoyance that Lee had helped himself to his best bottle. Robbie had kept it sealed, nestled in its smart blue silk-lined presentation box, saving it for a special occasion. From the sway of Lee's walk, Robbie could see that he had managed to pour himself most of the bottle already, without the assistance of anyone else. He was a large, muscular man, with a good tolerance for alcohol, but the whisky had hit its mark, slowing him and slightly slurring his speech.

Robbie was caught off guard when Lee put down his glass and hugged him suddenly, pulling him too close. The whisky bottle still clutched in Robbie's hand made the hug even more awkward, but Lee didn't seem to notice. Jesus, was he crying? Robbie was unsure what to do, so just patted him lightly on the back with his free hand. Lee pulled back, wiping snot and tears on the backs of his hands, babbling something Robbie couldn't quite decipher.

Slumping back down into Robbie's favourite leather reclining chair, he told him to fetch a glass for himself, as he didn't want to drink alone. Robbie went obediently to the kitchen area, making a mental note to clear the mess of broken glass later. He returned with a tumbler. Whisky wasn't his usual drink of choice. He had never tasted Blue Label before, but knew it was expensive. He imagined it must be a cut above the cheaper stuff. Taking a sip, the whisky immediately burned his throat, stung his eyes and caused him to cough. *Disappointing*, he thought. Lee managed a half-laugh at Robbie's discomfort and pointed to a chair.

Oh god, thought Robbie. It looked like Lee wanted to have a heart to heart. He preferred angry, psychopathic Lee to this version. He wanted to ask where he had been, but he didn't want to say anything which might wind him up and make him more dangerous. Sitting down, keeping his eyes on the dram in his glass, Robbie waited for Lee to speak.

Clearing his throat, Lee began. 'I'm going to tell you something, and I guarantee I'll kill you if you repeat it to anyone. Do you understand?'

Robbie gulped, his eyes went wide, his ears started ringing and his cheeks flamed. *If only you knew*, he thought, *that you're probably telling the whole CID*. Robbie didn't know where the bugs in his flat had been hidden and now he was glad of it. He imagined they were everywhere. His eyes roamed the room, as he tried to swallow down panic with the harsh taste of whisky. He hoped the police were listening. At least if Lee came at him, deciding to kill him after all, the police might be able to kick down the door and help him.

Robbie assumed that Lee was about to share with him the grizzly details of the murder he had committed and was still on the run for. Steeling himself, he mentally prepared to hear about stabbing, blood spill, pleading and all the other details which would fuel his future nightmares. He was still thinking about this as he became aware that Lee was talking, but his words didn't match what he had expected to hear.

Robbie's mouth was dry. He could feel the effect of the alcohol already slowing his brain, as he struggled to process Lee's words.

'Not my father.'

As if operating on a satellite delay, Robbie slowly caught up with Lee's disclosure. Ralph Aitchison was not his father. His uncle John was his dad, but that didn't make sense. Seeing incomprehension on Robbie's face, Lee spelled it out for him, spitting out words as if they were poison in his mouth, 'My ma's brother is my dad.'

Robbie was dumbstruck. He couldn't find any suitable words and then was too scared to say anything at all. He kept his mouth shut and his eyes on Lee, too frightened even to blink in case it caused Lee to suddenly flip out.

The weight of Lee's eyes on him eventually made Robbie break his silence.

'That wee junkie. He knew?' Robbie said, adding unnecessarily, 'The boy you killed?'

Lee swallowed a mouthful of whisky and nodded. 'Said my uncle John told him. I think I already knew deep down. His *special* visits when I was a bairn. My dad running scared of him. Christ! My mum scared of him but running after him. I think he only did it to my mum to show her and the old man that he could do whatever he wanted. A sick power trip. He's scum and my old man should have stopped it.'

Robbie felt like a goldfish, his mouth opening and closing silently. To shut him up, Lee had killed the hopeless heroin addict, whose biggest mistake had been trying to extort some cash from him, to buy his silence. Now that Robbie knew Lee's secret, he realised the perilous position it placed him in. Robbie's eyes searched the room again. He had forgotten all about the bugs, and now was checking for anything Lee could use as a weapon against him in case he decided to end his confessional session violently.

Lee got to his feet and Robbie felt panic rise in his chest.

'What you doing now?' he asked Lee.

'Going to find the old man and kill him,' Lee told him levelly.

'John?' asked Robbie.

'No, the fuckin' sap who let it happen. I'll sort John later. You're driving me to Ralph's,' Lee said, draining his tumbler. Robbie wondered again how Lee's mind worked. It seemed that he was most annoyed with Ralph Aitchison about the whole matter, more than his uncle, and what about his mother? This was not good, this was not good at all, but he knew better than to resist Lee. Grabbing his car keys, he followed helplessly behind Lee and made for the door.

31.

Ralph Aitchison paced backwards and forwards, outside the roller-door entrance of his newly acquired industrial unit. Two of his men stood nearby, leaning against the brick wall, smoking and scrolling idly through mobile phones. Checking his watch again and looking towards the entrance of the small industrial estate, Ralph Aitchison kicked small stones in frustration. Eight minutes late. Where the hell was the wagon with his cocaine? With every passing minute his mind raced, inventing possible reasons for the delay. Maybe the driver had got wind of what he was carrying, and had just driven off with his haul? Maybe the Dutchman had double-crossed him and there was no haul? Maybe the Dutchman had shopped him to the Old Bill? Maybe Customs had done a spot check at Aberdeen harbour and found it? Maybe… Wait, here it was. About bloody time.

Aitchison's men stepped forward, ready to unload the approaching 7.5-tonne lorry. Ralph mimed to the driver to wait until the roller-doors were lifted and he gave a thumbs-up reply of compliance. There was no point in advertising what was going on here. The neighbours were already too nosey for his liking. He would be careful even though their units remained closed and there was no sign of them yet. Ralph wondered fleetingly where they were, but he was glad to have privacy at least. As he looked on, the driver noisily dropped the tail lift of the truck and rattled open the tailgate. Peering inside, Ralph saw a collection of anonymous, wooden packing crates, reinforced with metal strips. Each was painted with the word 'fragile' and could have contained anything. Pieces of curly wood shavings poked from the crates, protecting the contents. The men got straight to work with the forklift, unloading them, stacking them inside the unit and knowing better than to ask any questions.

Ralph Aitchison's phone rang. He checked the screen but didn't answer the call. He replaced the phone in his pocket, letting it ring out. The club could wait. He was busy. When his phone rang for a third time, as he was trying to prise open one of the crates and inspect the contents, he swore in frustration. Setting a tyre lever on top of the crate, he accepted the call, barking, 'What?'

A female voice at the other end told him that the alarm had gone off at the club and that it wouldn't reset. Could he swing past and look at it or did he want her to call out an engineer? He told her that he was busy, but then thought the better of it. Bloody typical of Lee to be missing in action, leaving everything to him. Checking a trouser pocket, he felt the bunch of keys he carried for the club. He could probably shut it off at least. Weighing his options, Ralph realised that he would make it there well before any engineer could respond, and he wanted the racket stopped before the police were dispatched to check it out. He could do without them roaming through his club.

Cursing, he told her that he was on his way. Shouting to his men, Ralph told them that he had an emergency to deal with at the club. He told them to carry on unloading the truck, to lock the unit behind them and call him when they were done. He asked them to hang about, parked up outside, keeping an eye on the place until he got back. The alarm would be a quick fix, he hoped, then he could return to the unit and get on with things. Why did nothing ever seem to run smoothly? It seemed that none of his plans ever did these days. He was losing his touch, or maybe it was just the anticipation of finally getting out.

Ralph Aitchison got behind the wheel of his black Mercedes, still swearing. Driving off, he wrestled with the seatbelt buckle, plugging it in to stop the infernal *ding-ding*. As he joined the dual carriageway heading to the city he was unaware of the unmarked firearms units heading towards the unit at speed.

Ralph's phone rang again. The car system answered it for him at the touch of a button. It was one of the lads he had just left at the unit. *That was quick*, he thought, as the call connected. Before he could say anything, he heard a clatter as the man's phone hit the concrete floor. At the same time, he heard a loud voice: 'Armed police! Get down!'

Aitchison's eyes bulged and he held his breath. He ended the call and braked hard, pulling over at the side of the road. He opened the driver's door just in time before he vomited on the carriageway. A white van swerved around his stationary car with its horn blaring. Ralph ignored it and vomited again. This time only bile and stringy saliva came up as he realised what disaster had befallen him. Wiping his mouth on the back of his hand, he drove numbly towards the club, calculating how much cash he had in the safe there, and feeling sick again when he realised that it amounted to not much more than the price of a decent second-hand car. His passport was in the safe, and like it or not, he had already pressed the eject button. There would be no pot of gold for his retirement plan, only survival mattered now. Still tasting vomit in his mouth, he pressed harder on the accelerator pedal. Time was running out.

32.

Lucy had settled into her holiday on Tiree after the shaky start. She was still experiencing disturbed sleep and nightmares, but when she woke in the middle of the night in the bothy, frightened, tired and listless, the fear left her more easily when she got up, made a cup of tea and sat looking out onto the peaceful night landscape of clouds passing across the moon and its reflection on the sea.

Awake again in the middle of the night, Lucy poured hot water over one of the herbal teabags which had been in the welcome hamper, leaving it to bob about in her mug. She pulled on a sweatshirt and padded outside to sit on the wooden front step, peering through the darkness towards the sound of the waves. Salty water, seaweed and the camomile tea soothed her senses. She inhaled gratefully and deeply, her heartbeat slowing, her mind clearing and her mood lifting. She saw wave crests highlighted by the bright moon, miles out to sea. Closer to her, foamy white water was lifted on gentle waves and deposited on to the sandy shoreline. It was still and quiet. She could hear the swoosh of water over the slight cool breeze. Lucy didn't have many days left on the island and was determined to memorise as many of the sights and sounds as she could, searing happy memories on to her brain.

The holiday had done her the power of good. She felt more rested than she could remember being in a long time. Her limbs were tanned and toned from long hot walks, followed by cold swims in the clear blue sea. It was far better than any gym. Her mental health was improving with the rest, the exercise and the freedom afforded to her on the island. Even her tastebuds seemed to have woken up and to have changed. She had developed a liking for the herbal teas Kathy had introduced her to; the same ones she had previously considered bags of potpourri dust. Back inside, she placed the empty mug at the sink, and stretched. Yawning, she checked the teabag situation, deciding to buy some more supplies in the morning. Back in bed, Lucy nestled under the covers, closed her eyes, and quickly fell into a dreamless sleep.

Early the next morning, Lucy sat on the front step, with a fresh cup of tea. She rooted through her big black rucksack, finding the tiny notebook which she had bought on a previous expedition to the shops. Hobson's choice had made her the owner of the notebook with its front cover of a roller-skating rodent. Its cartoonish face was pink with exertion and its mouth formed a perfect 'o' as it fought for balance. With her pen at the ready, Lucy flipped open the book and made a short shopping list.

Checking the back of the notebook, her fingers trailed down a list of dates and times, from the past and in the future. They were a series of telephone-consultation appointments with Norma, her trauma therapist. She had been exceptionally glad of Norma's guidance and support after the story had been published in a national Sunday newspaper. Thankfully, there had been no more sneaky visits from journalists to Lucy's parents' house, and they had probably given up on her empty flat by now. She had been absolutely mortified to see her name in print. The story had been sensationalised, as she had expected. At least they didn't have a photograph of her, so perhaps she could continue with her surveillance career when things settled down.

Danny would have been livid. There would be no doubt that he would have read the article which branded him a 'love rat' and had a photograph of his snarling face splashed across the page. The article had been scathing about him and she shivered unconsciously, imagining him reading the paper.

Lucy was due to meet her counsellor for her first face-to-face session when she returned from holiday. She already felt the benefit of their telephone sessions, sure they were aiding her sleep. Norma had given her permission to grieve the broken relationship, and the breach of her trust, to be sad about it and to be gentle on herself until she could process it and move on. She had explained to Lucy that it was perfectly natural that her sleep pattern was disturbed. She encouraged her to take naps throughout the day if she felt the need. She had also told her that when she lay in bed unable to sleep, she should resist checking the time.

When she rose in the morning and felt bad about how little sleep she had managed, Lucy should instead tell herself that she had managed to bank 'sufficient sleep for the day'. She had been sceptical at first, but it was working. Before that, Lucy had been surviving on only a handful of hours' sleep, but now she was beginning to thrive. Her thought process was sharper and the brain fog was disappearing. Norma gave her coping strategies to use for her nightmares and for panic attacks in case she had another.

With her shopping list complete, Lucy sat next to the rucksack, noticing that it had taken on a new smell. She sniffed it, the straps had absorbed the unmistakeable sweet coconut of her suntan lotion from previous hikes. It was in happy contrast to its stark appearance. Tapping the pen on her teeth in contemplation, Lucy wondered what she could buy Kathy to leave behind as a special thank-you present. She had seen some small bunches of carnations in the Spar shop but felt that she deserved more. She hadn't found a florist on the island, but perhaps she could ask at the village today on her walk. Lucy ripped a page from her notebook, scribbled a short note and left it under the smooth stone perched on the step – a 'sea-mail' in case Kathy should call round, letting her know she had gone out walking. Checking her digital watch, Lucy added the time, then lifted her rucksack and set off.

33.

Ralph Aitchison had caused quite a stir on the fast drive to his club in Aberdeen city centre. He lost count of the number of angry horns which had sounded and punctuated his manoeuvres. Sweat beaded on his red face, despite the air-conditioning in his Mercedes. He could smell his own vomit. It made his eyes water and it seemed to be trapped in his nostrils, even after he had crunched a Polo mint.

His sole focus was now on escape. He couldn't care less if he never saw his miserable wife or his grasping son ever again. He was finished with them, as much as his business was finished. Thanks to the filth, he had lost everything. His house and all his cash had been gambled on that last, desperate deal, and he had taken a loan from John. He was destitute. If the police got to him before his brother-in-law, it would be lesser of two evils. He never wanted to see the inside of a cell again, and he knew that even prison walls couldn't keep him safe. He was as good as dead already.

He had no Plan B. The only solution his desperate mind could conjure was to grab his passport and escape with whatever pittance of cash was left at the club. He would empty the safe and head straight to the airport. He would fly to the furthest away destination. In fact, he would just get on the first flight, wherever it was headed. Ralph parked round the corner from the club. There was no point in advertising his presence, even if he only intended to grab and go before the cops came looking for him. Glancing nervously over his shoulder, Ralph ducked into the darkness of the club and the shrieking alarm. He could smell stale alcohol on damp carpet mingled with artificial fruit from the grip spray used by the performers on the poles. It did nothing to aid his weak stomach.

He strode past a cleaner who was busy vacuuming sticky carpet in the seating area. She was wearing headphones and gave no sign of having registered his presence. He wondered how she could hear her music even with headphones, above the shrill din of the alarm system. The pitch made his developing headache worse, his temples seemed to pulsate in time with the wailing. Making his way directly to the small office, Ralph opened a control panel and slotted home a key. He punched in some numbers until, mercifully, the alarm stopped ringing. A persistent flashing light on the control panel let him know that it would probably only be a temporary fix. An engineer would need to be called out. *Not my problem*, thought Ralph, turning to find the cleaner hovering about the doorway with a big, stupid smile on her face and still wearing the headphones. Ralph stared at her. He had no idea where the cleaner hailed from, but looking at her beaming face and thumbs held aloft in triumph, he assumed with relief that she did not speak English. Ralph had no time for chit-chat. He didn't return the smile but managed a weak thumbs-up in reply before he mimed a 'shoo' motion to dismiss her, and the smiling cleaner disappeared.

Shrugging off his jacket, Ralph rooted through the top drawer of his office desk. He opened a small glass-fronted fridge, removed a bottle of water and gulped it down greedily. Leaving the half-empty bottle on his desk, Ralph turned to the safe, not wanting to waste any time. He had it open in seconds. His hands grappled inside, pulling all the contents to the front, then piling them on his desk. Ralph located his passport and shoved it in the back pocket of his suit trousers. He ripped open wage envelopes, tipped out their contents and heaped all the cash together. He still had his back to the door as he pawed through the notes, working out how much he had, when he heard the unmistakeable voice of his son, Lee, shouting at the cleaner to get out of his way.

Ralph's pulse quickened. Retrieving his suit jacket, he quickly began to stuff cash into the pockets. He sat down at his desk, facing the door, opening another drawer, rooting around inside it for anything else that he might be able to use or sell. *Jesus, Lee had finally decided to show his face, now of all times! Typical!* thought Ralph. *Never there when he needed him and then always in the way.*

He hoped that Lee had not been tipped off about the drugs bust yet. He would have to play it cool; Lee couldn't know that he was leaving. His body started to shake with nervous tension. He needed to run, but now he was going to be even more delayed, effectively tethered to the swivel chair at his executive desk. Ralph had time to grab a bottle of whisky from the open drawer and was reaching for a couple of tumblers when Lee barged through the door.

Ralph tried to give the impression that he had been there all morning and was in no particular rush. Looking up at Lee as he entered the office, he could see that he was infuriated. Lee stood in front of the desk, with his arms by his side and his fists pumping. He looked glassy-eyed and he reeked of booze. He stood, swaying slightly in front of him, livid. Veins pulsed in his neck and at his temples under close cropped hair. Ralph swallowed his own fear, thinking that Lee must have somehow found out about the deal gone wrong. Forcing himself to be the boss, he met Lee's eyes.

'I was going to offer you a drink, but it looks like you've had enough already,' Ralph said.

He willed his hands not to shake, as he poured himself a generous measure and took a large swig, using it to wash the last of the vomit from his mouth. He swallowed, still looking at his angry son, waiting for him to speak and formulating what he could say to save his skin.

Robbie Gillies entered the office and stood inside the doorway, his downcast eyes studying the swirled pattern of the red carpet. Lee leaned over the desk, taking the tumbler of whisky from Ralph's hand, swallowing some before gathering himself to his full, menacing height. Ralph sat back in his chair, with his hands on the edge of the large dark wood desk. The deep polished surface was scuffed and ringed with the ghosts of hundreds of cups and glasses from the years he had owned it. Still eyeing Lee, Ralph's hands moved slowly and deliberately along the edge of his desk. His right hand searching for the catch he knew was there. The hidden mechanism had delighted Ralph in a childish way and had been the reason he chose the desk. A perfect hidey hole for something small, something important.

'Where the hell have you been?' Ralph asked him, speaking louder than necessary to cover his nerves and the soft click of the compartment's release. Moving his hands onto his lap, Ralph played for time, wishing he had a magician's sleight of hand, but reckoning that his son's alcohol stupor would suffice.

'Listen, son, if it's money you need—' Ralph started.

'*Son!*' The word exploded from Lee's mouth. His red

eyes brimmed with fire and hate.

'*You* are no father of mine,' spat Lee, taking a step closer to the desk again. He raised his hands in a boxer's stance, ready to fight.

Ralph was confused. If it wasn't the deal, what had made his son so psychopathically angry? Something was dangerously wrong with him. Robbie stood still in the doorway, trying not to look at the hammer protruding from Lee's waistband as Lee moved a hand behind his back, ready to pull it out.

'The place is crawling with cops,' Ralph tried again, playing for time, like a child at bedtime. 'I'll take you away, get you on a plane somewhere,' he tried to reason.

'You pathetic piece of shit,' Lee laughed. A humourless, menacing sound, which caused Robbie to squirm. 'Uncle John is my dad!' Lee blazed.

Ralph steadied himself, as if he had just been punched. His mouth opened wordlessly.

'You knew!' Lee spat, 'and you did nothing. You let him screw your wife, swan about. You were too frightened of him!' Lee shouted.

Ralph felt bile rise again within him. 'How?' was all that he managed to utter.

'That wee junkie,' Lee told him.

Ralph thought back, remembering the killing. It had been so out of character, so unnecessary for Lee to stab the hapless addict. It had been a frenzied attack but now it made sense. He had somehow known, and he had made the mistake of telling Lee. Jesus!

Lee flew at Ralph, with the claw hammer held aloft, his face a mask of white-hot anger. At that moment, Ralph showed his right hand, which held a Glock 17, 9mm, self-loading pistol, its internal striker already cocked and ready to fire.

Robbie felt a fine mist of moisture settle on his face and clothes, as Lee was knocked backwards off his feet, a boxer taking a lethal blow. The hammer fell from Lee's hand, and a small hole appeared in his chest. Robbie saw a gaping hole, in the centre of Lee's back, dark and leaking blood, less than a second before he hit the carpet. He felt his ears ring from the sudden explosion of the round as it found its target, sound waves rattling through the office. Covering his ears, a second too late, a small, animal noise escaped Robbie's mouth as he registered that it was Lee's blood, not rain which had lightly pattered onto him. The room was suddenly drenched with the metallic smell of fresh blood mixed with too much aftershave. It made him immediately nauseous. Eyes round and glassy with shock, Robbie looked at Ralph, thinking that he was bound to be next for a bullet. Robbie raised both of his hands in surrender, mouth working, trying to plead for his life but no words would come out.

Ralph's eyes fixed on Robbie's. A small smile of resignation played on his lips. He looked calmer than he had ever seen him, which only added to Robbie's terror. The dark red of Lee's blood seeped into the crimson carpet, blurring the pattern of swirls and inching closer to Robbie's blood-splattered, new white trainers. Ralph moved the Glock towards himself, closed his eyes, tipped his head back, placed the still-hot muzzle under his clean-shaven chin and pulled the trigger. Another massive bang and soundwaves bounced round the office as Robbie, helpless and dumb, stood watching.

Deafened, and in a state of total shock, Robbie looked at Ralph's lifeless figure. His mind kept replaying the backwards rock then forward slump before Ralph landed on his desk. With his eyes blinking rapidly, Robbie moved sideways, towards the doorway. He kept looking at Lee's dead body, half-expecting him to get back on his feet in a hail of expletives.

34.

Lucy was walking past An Talla, a community centre on the island of Tiree, when her attention was drawn to a small red van which was parked outside, next to the entrance. The side door of the van was open, showing several large bundles of beautiful yellow and white roses inside.

Lucy walked up a slope, towards it. As she approached the van, she was unable to resist stepping close enough to inhale the warm, heady aroma of roses.

'Can I help you?' a woman in her mid-forties with long brown hair hanging over the shoulders of a blue linen smock, asked.

'I was looking for a florist. I haven't found one yet on the island and I'd like to send flowers to someone.' Lucy said self-consciously, feeling hot and sweaty from the walk. She could feel damp patches on the back of her t-shirt where the rucksack sat snugly against her, providing a layer of insulation that she didn't need. Her wind-swept hair was frizzy and knotted.

The woman explained that she was setting up the hall for a wedding. Lucy offered to help her carry some of the flowers into the hall and she accepted gratefully. They talked as they walked into a large airy hall with wooden ceilings.

Lucy suspected that the simple, multipurpose hall was usually a sparse affair, but as her eyes adjusted to the darkness of the cool interior, she saw that it had been transformed into a magical place. Fairy lights twinkled from rafters, and tables and chairs were set up, decked with starched white linen. Golden ribbon was tied in bows and hung from the backs of chairs. Candles floated in shallow dishes, surrounded by posies of yellow and white roses on each table. It smelled and looked heavenly.

'Wow,' Lucy said, admiring the scene.

'Thanks,' the florist told her, with a warm smile. 'I can't take all of the credit though.'

Lucy explained that she wanted to surprise Kathy with a special arrangement before she left. The florist beamed at the mention of her name, 'I know Kathy. She's a great artist.'

Lucy agreed, digging out her purse to pay for flowers to be delivered to Kathy. Declining the offer of a lift, Lucy helped carry the remaining flowers from the van before setting off again on foot to the nearby shop.

By the time she entered the Spar, Lucy was sweating again. Picking up a basket, she checked her shopping list. Her mobile vibrated in the pocket of her shorts with a series of incoming text messages and voicemail alerts. Lucy felt herself jolt to a stop. The trigger of the phone vibration caused uninvited images to swim before her eyes. Her heart thumped harder and faster in her chest, and her breathing became quick and shallow. She felt like her throat was being squeezed and she became uncomfortably hot. She lost peripheral vision, feeling suddenly dizzy and weak. She felt as if she was dying.

Recognising the symptoms as a panic attack, Lucy fought to remember her therapist Norma's advice. She forced herself to focus on one thing. Her eyes locked on a tray of Golden

Delicious apples. Concentrating on one, she examined it carefully, looking at the honey colour, picking out tiny brown flecks on the skin, seeing the twiglike, rough texture of the brown, stubby stalk. Lucy replaced the unwanted images with the apple, slowly regaining control of her breathing, making herself slow it down, counting inwardly as she inhaled, held her breath, then exhaled.

Bright white sparks which had begun to creep into the edges of her vision faded, and she heard the chatter of a radio DJ announcing a song. Lucy blinked away tears, set down the basket, stood up straight and exhaled audibly. Thank god, she had managed to hold it together. She didn't want to make a spectacle of herself in the shop. She picked the basket back up, feeling the dreaded buzz of the phone again. This time she was ready for it, accepting that it was just a message. 'Don't panic!' Lucy told herself. She consciously acknowledged that her phone had received a message, but told herself that it would wait until she decided to read it. Making herself concentrate on the shopping list instead, she felt shaky but proud of herself in a small way. Slowly she was recovering from Danny's grasp and the fear that he had instilled within her. She wouldn't allow herself to be tortured by a mobile phone.

Picking up a box of teabags, Lucy was relieved that she had been able to bring herself back from the grip of panic. Her legs were still wobbly, but she got stronger with every step round the shop. Her phone began to vibrate persistently, an incoming call, but she was able to keep it in the background, to function normally. As if to prove a point to herself, Lucy deliberately took her time, browsing the small freezer containing frozen lollies and ice creams. Smiling inwardly at the small victory, she decided to reward herself with a choc ice which she could eat on the beach across the road from the shop.

Lucy packed groceries in her rucksack, ignoring the enquiring black-rimmed eyes of the young shop assistant who obviously wondered why she was ignoring the noticeably buzzing mobile phone in her pocket. She pulled the wrapper off her ice cream and asked the shop assistant to dispose of it for her.

Walking back outside into the sun, Lucy crossed the empty road towards a stony outcrop on the white sand, to sit and enjoy her ice cream. The wind whipped strands of her hair into her mouth as she ate, but it was delicious. She concentrated on the taste, watching a bird wading in and out of the shallows, dodging waves as they crept up the sand. The sea was a sparkling palette of blues from navy to aquamarine. Salty air filled her lungs as she breathed slowly and deeply before pulling the mobile phone from her pocket.

Holding it in front of her, Lucy scrolled through a string of missed calls, voicemail alerts and texts. Unsurprisingly, most of the numbers were unknown or withheld, which Lucy expected would be Danny hiding behind new digits. She didn't doubt that he would be all over the voicemail messages too. He knew that he was calling her police-issued phone, was well aware of the consequences, but was still unable to cut contact with her. She wouldn't be returning any of the messages or calls. Lucy was aware of tightness in her throat and felt her heart rate increase, but she concluded that she was okay. She could cope with this. Despite being miles from home, in a remote location, she still scanned the area all around herself, but saw only birds on the empty beach. 'He's not here,' she told herself, 'It's okay.'

Lucy checked the messages; they had all arrived in a tumble when she was in the shop and the patchy phone signal had eventually connected. Some of the messages were from her DS, Chris Summers. She read them first. Her eyes widened, and she got to her feet in astonishment. She read the same message three times before allowing herself to believe it.

Ralph and Lee Aitchison were dead. A murder-suicide at the club. A million pounds worth of cocaine had been seized. Lee was the product of incest. What the hell? She had been away for less than a fortnight, and the family behind one of the biggest organised crime groups had imploded. Good grief! She was disappointed and relieved not to have been involved in the last stages of Operation Flame. Knowing that any part she would have been allowed to play would have been in the back office, and well away from the action, eased the feeling of having missed out.

She would call Chris later, hungry for all the details. She imagined that he would be busy just now and it could wait. She would be back at the office in a few days anyway. Trying to hold on to the new feeling of calm and control, Lucy steeled herself to open the text messages and voicemails which she assumed were from Danny.

35.

Sitting back down on the most comfortable of the uncomfortable rocks, Lucy shielded her screen from bright sunlight to better read the text messages. She felt the familiar heavy weight return in her stomach but consciously maintained control of her senses. They were all from Danny.

It's Danny. Call me X
Call me, now X
Why won't you call me? XX
It's urgent, Call me X
Please. I'm begging. Call me X
Where are you?
????????
Where the hell are you? You're not at work.
Are you with someone?
Where are you? I just want to talk.
Didn't take you long to move on I guess.
Are you with him now?
You fucking slut.
I hope you're happy now.
You ruined my life, you slut.
Fucking slut. I hope you die.
Fuck You.
Please just call me X

Where are you? Not at work. You at home?

Lucy struggled to remain composed as she worked her way through the list of increasingly agitated messages. Her palms were sweaty, and a chill crept up her back, despite the warm air. The beach noises began to fade away until Lucy was aware of only the sound of her own pulse in her ears. He had a new number and he was still pestering her.

Lucy steadied her breathing, focussed on the job in hand and reminded herself that she was safe. He wouldn't know where she was. A message from another new number was next. She assumed that Danny was behind it too, but the message was set out differently from his. The words and the format used were different. She read it twice, looking for a trap, worried that it might be Danny after all.

Lucy, this is Paul. Sorry to bother you. I'm Danny's friend. Danny has totally lost it. I hope you're OK. Please keep safe. Have you seen him? Do you know where he is? I'm really worried about him.

She was reluctant to engage in text conversation in case Danny was lurking behind it. It had a genuine ring of truth about it and the '*please keep safe*' gave her cause for concern. As she considered whether or not she should reply, the phone began to buzz in her hands with an incoming call from the same number. Paul? Should she answer it? Before she could change her mind, she swiped at the screen to accept the call. She remained silent, waiting to hear the caller's voice before she spoke, to ensure that it was not Danny. The wind made it difficult to hear, so she covered her other ear with her free hand. A male voice which was definitely not Danny's said, 'Hello? Hello, is that Lucy? Lucy, it's Paul. Can you hear me?'

Lucy took a second to reply, 'Yes. What's happened?'

Paul began to speak so quickly that she had difficulty keeping up. After having an 'episode', Danny had taken off and was now missing. He had taken pills and a bottle of whisky with him and had driven off. Paul didn't know where he was, but suspected that he would go to Lucy.

'Has he actually taken the pills?' Lucy asked, thinking back to the night he had disappeared when they were at his brother's house, re-emerging to mock their concern and tell them that he had been watching the search for him. She shivered at the memory.

'He took them with him. I don't know if he has had any yet, I can't be sure.'

'What did he do?' she asked, unsure if she was ready to hear the answer.

'He went berserk apparently. Punched and kicked holes in the wall, the doors. He smashed his house up. The cops are looking for him.'

Lucy swallowed hard. 'Did he hurt Susan?' she asked, already suspecting that she knew the answer.

'Yes. It's bad, Lucy. Luckily their neighbour came round and stopped it. He phoned for an ambulance and the police came too.'

Lucy couldn't speak. Goosebumps ran up her body to her face as she imagined the scene, and it brought back unwanted memories.

'Is she alive?' she asked, gripping the phone tightly.

'Yes, but she's in a really bad way. My wife's at the hospital, waiting for news. I dropped the kids off at their grandparents, and now I'm out looking for him. Where do you think he'll go?'

Lucy found that she was standing again, searching all round her, on red alert, half-expecting to see him appear from behind a rock, out for revenge on her before he killed himself. Fighting the urge to run, Lucy willed herself to keep the panic down, not to let it fill her head and body.

Her voice was strangled as she told Paul, 'He messaged me. I think he left voicemails too, but I don't know where he is.'

Instinct told Lucy not to disclose her whereabouts to Paul. Just in case Danny was listening in or would find out.

'I'm not at home right now,' was all that she offered.

'I'm driving to your place now,' Paul told her. 'Can I meet you there?'

'No!' she almost shouted the response. Even if she was not several miles and a ferry trip away from the flat, there was nothing she wanted less than to be there now, to be a sitting duck.

'Okay. I understand. Please let me know if you hear from him. You can reach me on this number,' Paul said hurriedly, before hanging up.

Adrenaline pumped through Lucy's body and every nerve fired. She wanted to run and hide, but fought the urge. The logical part of her brain told her it wouldn't help. She channelled the focus that Norma had taught her.

'Think! Think, Lucy!' she told herself aloud.

With shaking hands, she dialled to hear the voicemail messages from Danny, dreading what might be waiting for her, but knowing she needed to find out. Her skin prickled and her blood ran cold as she listened to his voice, barely audible at times, above the background noise of car tyres on tarmac, engine sounds and the wind rushing past. His voice held her tight in fear, but she made herself keep listening, trying to pick up any clues as to where he might be. He was driving and it sounded like he was moving fast.

His voice sounded flat. Too calm in comparison with his text messages and for someone who had done what

Paul had described. It had a petrifying effect, rooting her to the spot.

'Hello, Lucy. I hope you're doing well. You have totally fucked up my life. I hope you're happy now. I thought we had a future together. I was going to take you back.'

Her ears began to hum and her own shallow panting made it difficult for Lucy to hear the quietly spoken words above road noise.

Danny went on, 'You've made it very clear that you don't want me. I'm coming to see you. We need to talk and you're going to listen to me. We're going to talk about you grassing me up. You owe me that at least. Who are you seeing now? It didn't take you long to move on, did it? You bitch.'

The last word sounded like it was uttered through gritted teeth, measured and menacing. Lucy sat down on the rocks, fingers in her mouth, eyes darting about and unable to end the call or to pull the handset away from her ear. 'Oh god', he was looking for her. Did he know where she was? It sounded as if he did. Was he on his way here? Where could she hide? Would the teenage girl in the Spar with the heavy eye make-up let her hide in the storeroom? Lucy's eyes pictured herself in a dark room, with the smell of cardboard boxes and dust around her, cowering silently in a corner while Danny searched for her.

'Concentrate!' she told herself, recognising that she was beginning to spiral towards a panic attack. She thought she might faint but she fought back, making herself focus on her right foot, noticing all the detail. A brown, dark leather walking boot, scuffed and worn at the black rubber toe cap. A red lace, tied in a double knot, one end frayed.

'Breathe. Just breathe. This is important,' she coached herself. Holding a ragged breath for three seconds, Lucy fought for control, holding back the wave of panic.

Feeling hot and shaky, but holding on to strong determination, Lucy played back the voicemail message from Danny, listening carefully to the part that she had missed when she had begun to shut down.

'You've fucked up your own job too. I was in the newspapers. My fucking name, my picture. Like some fucking criminal.' His voice had become louder, anger spilled into it. There was a shrillness in his tone now, a creeping mania.

'So, if I'm going to die, then so are you. You go first.' He let out a strangled cackle, then added, 'Ladies first. I'm coming for you, then I'm going to climb to the top of a hill and have a picnic. I've got pills and whisky for my picnic.'

Lucy forced herself to concentrate on background noises in the call. The car engine was still audible. Finally, the voicemail message must have reached capacity and cut him off. Lucy planned what to do next. Then she scrambled to her feet, put on her rucksack and started awkwardly running back over the beach, heading for the beacon of the small supermarket across the road. With her heart thumping, she played the next voicemail message from Danny, only able to hear every other word as she huffed urgently towards the shop.

The shop assistant's eyes bulged as Lucy stumbled into the shop, breathless and alarmingly agitated. Lucy saw that she was in her late teens. She wore the shop uniform's black polo shirt, trimmed with red, which suited her jet-black hair, white face, thick, black eye make-up and dark-purple lipstick. Her ears and nose were pierced, and her fingernails were bitten short and painted black. On her uniform shirt was a nametag which read 'Brenda'.

In the empty shop, Brenda took an involuntary step back as Lucy approached the counter with the big black rucksack still bobbing on her back and waving a mobile phone in the air. While she caught her breath, Lucy removed the rucksack and placed it on the floor, fishing inside it. Brenda wondered if she was about to be held up by the mad woman who was probably pulling out a weapon of some kind. Before she could work out whether she would hand over all the cash from the till or would try to overcome the lunatic, Lucy pulled out her notebook and placed it on the counter. Unable to locate her pen, Lucy saw a biro on top of a stack of invoices on a shelf behind Brenda and asked for it. Brenda complied, still wondering what was going on. Maybe the woman was going to write down her demands? Still recovering from the run up the beach, Lucy grabbed the pen and scribbled down her name and the address of her flat. On another sheet, she wrote Danny's name and his date of birth. Checking the call record on her mobile, Lucy wrote down the most recent number that Danny had used to call her.

'Phone 999,' Lucy told the surprisingly composed Brenda. 'I'm Lucy. I'm an off-duty police officer. That is my home address. This man,' she said, pointing to Danny's name, 'is on his way to my address. The police are looking for him. He's wanted for a serious assault or an attempted murder.'

Brenda's black-rimmed eyes widened even further. She spat out a wad of chewing gum into her hand in preparation to make the call. Brenda thought it was madness, but she had always known that she would be involved in something like this one day, and she was ready for it.

Brenda listened as Lucy explained, 'Use the landline. My phone signal is patchy but I'm going to use my mobile to try and speak to him.' Jabbing a finger at Danny's name on the page, Lucy continued, 'I need to find out exactly where he is to tell the police.'

Lucy looked into Brenda's gleaming eyes, asking her, 'Do you understand? This is important.'

'Yes,' Brenda replied quickly, wasting no time, turning to the grey plastic telephone fixed to the wall behind her, already pressing the first '9' of her call.

Lucy called Danny's number. Her heart was still hammering wildly, but from tension now, rather than the run. Danny answered on the second ring.

'Hello, Lucy. Where are you?'

Lucy swallowed and tried her best not to sound terrified. Her legs felt shaky, but she needed to know exactly where he was, and to keep him talking, hopefully until the police could get to him. She loathed him now. She had no positive feelings towards him whatsoever, but she couldn't allow him to know that. She needed to play his game.

She tried to sound compassionate, recalling a time when she had interviewed a man who had sexually abused a child. She had hidden her own feelings of revulsion, maintaining a cool, professional demeanour. She had controlled her emotions, careful not to let disgust or judgement creep into her voice, as he recounted his vile actions. He had confessed, giving her the information that she needed to secure a conviction, and to keep the public safe from him. He had whined, feeling sorry for himself, and ridiculously had blamed the victim for leading him on. She had been commended for the result, but she remembered vomiting as soon as the interview was over. She needed to keep the same mindset now – business first.

With her eyes closed, Lucy activated her police-work mode and composed herself. Able to think more clearly, she calculated that the road noise she had heard in the background of the recorded call suggested that his car was travelling at greater speed than the island's roads would support. He was on the mainland, driving on a motorway or dual carriageway section. Since it was highly unlikely that he knew where she was, but he knew she wasn't at work, Lucy assumed that he was probably on his way to look for her at the flat. If he had driven from Susan's house, he would have been on a motorway and then a dual carriageway. Guessing at the timings from the voicemail, he was likely to be on the dual carriageway section right now, the road noise suggested he was still moving fast enough, she thought.

'Where are you?' She asked him.

'Coming to get you,' he replied flatly.

She needed to confirm that he was heading for the flat. She could hear Brenda answering a series of questions, obviously speaking to an emergency call handler. She was doing well, and it gave Lucy a well-needed confidence boost, as she continued the call with Danny. She could hear that his car had slowed. There was less wind and road noise, and his voice was clearer now.

'I'm not at the flat just now. I'm at the shop,' Lucy told him. That much was true, she thought.

'Well, that's handy, 'cos I'm not far away. I can pick you up.'

Goosebumps crawled up Lucy's arm as she recoiled at the prospect.

'No, that's okay, I've got the car,' she told him, adding, 'I'll be as quick as I can and I'll see you in the car park.'

Lucy could no longer hear engine noise and she heard what sounded like a car door closing quietly as she had spoken. She could hear footsteps on a gritty pavement or road now. She guessed that he was out the car, walking towards her building.

An elderly man walked into the shop. He paid no attention to Lucy, and she wondered if Brenda might 'shoo' him out. But she appeared to be well-practised, keeping up her side of the '999' call conversation, jamming the receiver between her ear and her shoulder while ringing up payment for a newspaper. She handed back a few coins in change and gave a wave as he wandered out of the shop. Danny spoke again.

'Ah! So, you *are* at the shop. I thought you might be telling me lies, Lucy-Goosey,' he said sarcastically.

He must have heard the till in the background, Lucy realised, thanking her luck. She heard the distinct squeaking of the communal front door opening at Danny's end. So, he did still have a key for her flat! It shouldn't have been a surprise to Lucy – she had assumed that he would have had another key cut before he moved out, leaving his original key behind – but she was still annoyed by the audacity of it. She had considered oiling the squeaky hinge of the heavy front door, since she could hear it from inside her flat whenever anyone entered or left, but had decided to leave it for that very reason. It was one of her early warning traps round the flat. As Danny's voice echoed slightly in the hallway, Lucy reckoned that he was approaching her front door. She circled the address of her flat and gave an 'okay' hand signal for Brenda to give confirmation of his location to the call taker.

'Did you park in the front car park?' Lucy asked him, buying time.

'Yes. You'll just have to use the visitor's space,' Danny told her.

'Are you waiting in the car?' Lucy asked unnecessarily, but not wanting him to know that she was monitoring his movements. His voice echoed less now, and Lucy estimated that he was entering the hallway of her flat. She heard the telltale quiet tinkling sound as the small china bell that she kept behind the front door, was knocked over. Lucy heard him swear under his breath at his clumsy mistake. She felt

224

certain that he would take the opportunity to snoop around the whole flat. He would check for any sign that she had entertained anyone in his absence. He would find nothing, but he would still be suspicious and jealous. *Good*, she thought. *Keep searching. Be my guest and take your time*!

Lucy wrote again in the notebook – *He's inside the flat* – and Brenda relayed it to a police controller.

Brenda wrote back: *2 mins away*.

The police were closing in. The alarm they had left in the flat would have already sounded over their police radios, alerting them to the address, when Danny had failed to cancel it as soon as he entered the flat. There would be no audible sound inside the flat, but if Danny saw the set in the kitchen, he would immediately know what it was and might take off again. The police were on the way and, thanks to Brenda's updates, they had the full picture. They knew this was no false alarm.

'Has the car been running okay?' Lucy asked Danny.

She heard the kitchen utensil drawer open with its characteristic jangling of cutlery. *What did he want in there?* she asked herself.

Then almost immediately, the answer came to her, and she grabbed the notebook again, writing: *Knife?*

Brenda quietly relayed the message then wrote back: *Code*

Lucy didn't understand what she meant, but when she added *8-5*, she realised that it was the police alarm. The controller must have told her that there had been an activation. There would be even more officers en route now. Lucy was glad. She worried about the safety of those who were attending the call.

Suddenly a loud, male voice, steady and clear, rang through Lucy's flat and was broadcast through the phone in her hand.

'Police officer with a Taser! Stand still,' came the command.

Lucy heard shouting from Danny, other voices, scuffling, a chair falling over, then a loud shout from another officer, 'Knife!'

'Put the knife down,' he was commanded.

'Get back!'

Lucy heard more muffled shouting. Danny swore, then she heard a loud 'pop' and 'TASER! TASER!'

A childish scream came from Danny, then she heard the thump of his body as it hit the floor.

Brenda had terminated the call. The controller had told her that she could hang up when the police arrived. She was now concentrating fully on Lucy, trying to make sense of the commotion at the other end of the line.

Lucy heard the fast *tick-tick* of the Taser for several seconds before the police voice said, 'Handcuff under power'.

The *tick-tick* sound over silence seemed to last for a long time but was only seconds before the update followed.

'Subject secure.' The ticking stopped.

Lucy terminated the call with shaking hands. Her tense muscles relaxed and her legs felt like jelly. Adrenaline left her body as relief washed over her, leaving Lucy suddenly completely spent. Her shoulders dropped and her head fell forward as she slumped to the shop floor, sitting next to her rucksack with her back against the counter. Brenda came to her side, unscrewed the cap from a bottle of water and offered it to her. Lucy's whole body was shaking so much that Brenda had to help her steer the bottle to her lips. After a few moments, Brenda asked her if she was okay and if she could get her anything else.

'No, thanks.' Lucy said, giving her a tired smile.

Then she asked, 'What's your real name?'

'Brenda,' she shrugged and pointed to her name badge.

Lucy choked on a laugh, with a mouthful of water. Brenda started laughing too.

'I know!' she said.

36.

Lucy sat opposite the Detective Chief Superintendent at his tidy desk, sipping tea from a china cup. His office was plush with its pale blue painted walls, dark-blue carpet, brass desk lamp and matching framed family photographs. Lucy liked that he had hung the photographs on the walls, rather than have them on his desk. It was a bold statement that he was a happily committed, family man.

DCS Michael Atherton, was known to most of his staff by the nickname 'Cricket' and he was a good man. He'd had a long and successful police career, working his way up the ranks, gaining experience and respect as he went. He was a hard worker, but he was also a good boss with genuine interest in the welfare of his staff – a rare gem among the senior-ranking officers.

Placing his cup on its saucer, Mike looked at Lucy. He wore a sad smile as he asked her the usual welfare questions which Lucy answered politely and honestly.

'You've been through a hell of a time,' he stated, and she nodded in agreement.

'Are you absolutely sure you want to leave us?' he asked.

They both knew that Lucy had made her mind up to leave the CID. She felt that it was in her best interests, and he did too.

'I'm certain,' Lucy replied. 'Thanks for everything you've done for me. I really appreciate it.'

'It's not too late, you know?' he tried.

'I haven't rushed into this. I've taken my time. I've listened to good advice and I've carefully considered my options. I'm making the right move,' Lucy told him.

'What about somewhere different, still in CID? Fraud Squad? Intelligence?' he offered.

'No, thanks.' Lucy smiled, 'I have good memories from my time in the CID, but I'm moving on now.'

Mike got to his feet, offering his hand. Lucy rose to meet him, returning his hearty handshake. Shaking his head slowly, Mike told her, 'It's a great waste of a detective mind.'

Lucy smiled back, heading for the door to keep her appointment with stores for the fitting of her police uniform.

'I'm taking it with me, sir. I'm still going to use it!' she said.

Glad to leave the murky world of surveillance behind her, she was looking forward to the next part of her career and the adventures which lay ahead. She left his office with her head held high, a stronger person with the world at her feet again.

About the author:

N.M. Young

I started writing about fictional crime after a successful 30-year police career. Having a background in covert investigation and having dealt with numerous domestic abuse cases, I bring stories to life with understanding and passion.

Printed in Great Britain
by Amazon